Walking
Through Life
Without
Stumbling
Over Your Self

Walking Through Life Without Stumbling Over Your Self

By **Kathy Slamp**

ǔ

Published by Vessel Ministries, Wichita, Kansas.

Unless otherwise noted, Scripture quotations are from
New International Version.

ISBN 0-615-11148-3

Printed in the United States of America
2000

2500   6   SLA

<u>DEDICATION:</u>

To...

Dad and David—
Two great blessings in my life.
A wonderful father and a loving husband.
I honor you both!

OTHER BOOKS
BY KATHY SLAMP:

Reflection Profiles

Managing Women's Ministries

CONTENTS:

ACKNOWLEDGMENTS:

To my parents, J. Melton and Letitia Thomas,
for their initial "read" and their forever support.

To Lynn Baskerville
for his invaluable assistance with layout and format.

To Karen Baker
for editing the final copy.

To Joanne Wallace
for her inspiration and prayer support.

To Dr. Stan Toler
for his initial encouragment to begin this project.

TO THE READER:

Life is merely a composite of ordinary experiences in the lives of ordinary people. It really isn't the "big" things in life that cause us to stumble. It is a collection of the daily, ordinary events. Although many of the personal events I have shared in this book are not "little," some of them are small in light of eternity. The Bible says that it is the *"little foxes that spoil the vine."* Events of life come and go for all of us, and without His grace and mercy, we can allow our own "self" to get in His way. Then, any event of life could cause us to stumble and fall.

Walking Through Life Without Stumbling Over Yourself is written with the hope and prayer that you will begin to comprehend that God is in every happening of your life, and that each experience that comes through your life is a divine opportunity to prove Him and His Word. My prayer for you is that somehow, through these shared experiences, God can give you hope to face whatever circumstances may occur in your life. And that you can face whatever comes with joy and not stumble!

Chapter 1
My Favorite Day

Like most people I know, I have a favorite day of the year. For many people their favorite day of the year could be their birthday, their wedding anniversary, Christmas, or perhaps even the day some really significant event happened in their lives. My favorite day of the year is different from any one else that I know, for it is the last Saturday in October.

That particular Saturday is my favorite day because it is the twenty-five hour day—the day we set our clocks back one whole hour. Most people these days have lives as busy or busier than mine, and an extra hour is like a boon from heaven. Everywhere I go I'm promoting one of these days each month, and my campaign is actually catching on among many intelligent people.

A few years ago I was the chairperson of a statewide women's retreat; our committee had wisely selected my favorite day of the year to have this retreat. The retreat itself was to be one night and one day, and since women would be coming from the entire state of New Mexico and parts of extreme West Texas, we determined that having the retreat the last Saturday in October would be a great selling point. Halloween was concurrent with the last Saturday of October for that calendar. So that particular year my favorite day fell on October 31, Halloween.

The retreat had gone beautifully well, and we were all set to end with a banquet on Saturday night before the ladies returned in a dozen different directions to their homes. Our plans were to have the meal early in the evening, and because the clocks would all be set back, the women would still all get home at a reasonable hour. Right after noon that Saturday, we got reports that a snowstorm was heading our way. Since we were in the mountainous regions of New Mexico near Ruiodosa, we knew that we would need to adjust the schedule so that the women could get away ahead of the snow.

So we adjusted our schedule and moved everything back a couple hours. So far, so good! The speaker and I were to drive back together to my home in El Paso, Texas, where she was to speak the next morning at church and return home that afternoon. Since I was in charge of the entire retreat, she and I lingered behind a while, making sure all the ladies were safely departed and that cleanup crews were nearly done with their duties.

Shortly before five PM, she and I headed my car up out of the little valley where the retreat center was located. This was not new territory for me since our family had

made the trip numerous times; the weather was chilly, and the storm was near, but I was not frightened. I knew that once we made the twenty minute drive into Ruiodosa, we would head due west toward a little town called Tullarosa where we would turn due south and head home to

> *Basking in the spirit of a wonderful retreat, we set out, totally oblivious of the adventure and the miracle that lay ahead...*

El Paso. There was very little winter driving ahead for us; it was just a matter of getting ahead of the storm. Basking in the spirit of a wonderful retreat, we set out, totally oblivious of the adventure *and* the miracle that lay ahead during a night to remember.

The retreat center was hardly out of sight, however, before my passenger and I were aware that we were faced with a huge dilemma. Living in El Paso in the 1980s it was unbelievably "economical" to drive diesel automobiles since diesel fuel was between seventeen and twenty-three cents a gallon.

Like many El Paso residents, we, too, had a diesel car—which ran very well in warm weather. Detroit hadn't yet gotten all the "bugs" out of their cars, though, and one huge design flaw faced us that night; these cars didn't run too well in cold weather. Apparently, they had mistakenly placed a small air filter at the front of the radiator, and when cold air was pulled in, the filter would freeze, and then the car would stall. Such was our plight that night in October—October 31 to be exact—my favorite day of the year.

A trip that normally took about twenty minutes consumed nearly an hour. By the time we finally got into the little mountain town of Ruiodosa, it was dark, and we had started and stopped the car so many times that I knew we would never make it out of the cold weather. We stopped first at a gas station, for I had heard a "rumor" that a little gasoline would help diesel cars run better if they were having a problem. My better judgment got to me (thank goodness) before I put very much gasoline into the tank, and I decided that wasn't such a good idea. My passenger and I drove a couple blocks down the main street of Ruiodosa and finally stopped in the K-Mart parking lot under a huge light.

Why we stopped there, I'll never know. There we sat. Two women alone in the night! It was Halloween *and* my favorite day of the year; grown men and women were exiting K-Mart dressed in the strangest costumes. We would exchange glances, and it was difficult to tell which group thought the other was more weird. There we sat on a cold night not knowing what to do but knowing that there was no way under the sun that we could make it back to El Paso in our condition.

> *There we sat.*
> *Two women alone*
> *in the night!*

As we sat there under the light, a young man from El Paso who had been helping at the retreat drove by, saw us, and stopped. He asked the obvious: "Do you have a problem?" We were both tempted to respond with some cute reply about watching trick-or-treaters but decided that

he just might be our "angel of mercy." As much as I understood the problem, I explained our dilemma to him and told him our concerns about attempting the lonely journey across the desert under the circumstances. We checked the trunk and to our delight, my husband had a spare filter which our "angel" installed in a matter of minutes. I started the car, and it ran like a new sewing machine. With a wave and an optimistic grin, our young angel waved and disappeared toward El Paso.

We weren't in the least bit worried. After all, he had fixed the car; we were just "lucky" that he saw us, and in another three hours we would be safely home in El Paso. That wasn't the way it fleshed out, however. We left Ruiodosa heading due west across the desert on a desolate road toward Tullarosa.

The car sailed along smoothly for four or five miles, and then the unthinkable happened; the car began to chug and sputter and stall out just like it had done two hours earlier. I pulled over on the shoulder and attempted to drive as well as possible by starting and restarting the car every time it died. We were really alone now. No town for twenty-five miles. Few cars. Just my passenger and me!

Our retreat speaker looked at me at last and said, "Kathy, I think we had better pray." Interesting, isn't it? We had been in this dilemma for several hours now, and this was the first time we had prayed. Up until now, we had had a plan; there was someone to help us; or we had some idea what to do. Now we had exhausted our supply of ideas and resources.

We needed help! It was cold! It was dark! It was Halloween! It was scary! I turned to her and said, "About twenty miles down this road, there is a very little village. I know of a tiny church there, and if there is some way we can get this car there, we will park it, call El Paso, and wait in the one all night gas station until help arrives." That's the only solution I could think of, and in my mind it seemed utterly impossible.

As I drove on the shoulder, she began to pray: "Oh God," she prayed, "You know we are two women alone on the desert." (It always amuses me how we tell God what He already knows.) She continued, "God, you know that this car just isn't working right and that we can't afford to be stranded out here in the night alone. Oh God," she prayed, "help us get to..." At this point in her prayer she turned to me and addressed me rather than God: "Where is it we want to go?" she said. After I repeated to her that we needed to get to Tullarosa, she finished her prayer: "God, could you please just get us to Tullarosa."

Her prayer ended in a tone of desperation as she pleaded with God to intervene in our plight. Instantaneously, though, her tone changed from desperation to excitement for our car that was nearly stalled was beginning to pick up speed. "Kathy," she exclaimed excitedly, "God is answering our prayer."

"God is answering our prayer all right but not in the way you think," I responded. As my friend had prayed and I had watched, a miraculous thing had happened. The car began to pick up velocity even though the key was in the

off position, and I had NO power steering at all. When I pointed this out to my friend, and she saw for herself that the car was truly "off," she and I began to praise the Lord and rejoice at this absolutely unbelievable occurrence. Finally, I turned to her and said, "This is for the record." At that point, I took both hands off the steering wheel, turned around in the seat, and put my feet in her lap.

We were two women alone in the desert silently zooming through the night. We weren't alone, however, for like the three Hebrew children in the fiery furnace, there was a third presence with us, and that presence was *"like unto the Son of God."* There is

> ***There is no explaining how silent a car can be when God is driving it.***

no explaining how silent a car can be when God is driving it. There is no explaining the eerie feeling one gets to look behind the car and see no exhaust! There is no explaining the scary realization that God has a speed limit! Our car had begun to pick up speed and drive faster and faster, until it finally leveled off at 60 mph. (This was when mandatory speed limits were 55, and we both wondered what we would do if a patrolman tried to stop us.)

There are some challenges of faith when God is driving your car. This was not an unfamiliar road to me, and I was well aware that if God kept driving our car at 60 mph, we would soon be presented with at least one very big challenge. Before we ever got there, though, we were presented with one unexpected challenge—a slow moving vehicle in our lane! Generally, I am *automotively*

challenged, but it occurred to me that if I had no power steering, that the odds were quite high that I also had no power brakes. As we zoomed through the night, an extremely slow-moving farm vehicle pulled out in front of us. I reasoned that if God had gotten us this far, surely He could handle my steering, so manually I maneuvered the car around the slow vehicle and silently passed him in a quiet moonlit night.

My knowledge of the road ahead, however, concerned me immensely. I knew that the road into Tullarosa went directly west, took a right angle as it turned south, and then headed straight out through the desert toward El Paso. I also knew that at 60 mph the continual rejoicing and praising of my passenger would soon be turned to consternation as we attempted to negotiate an impossible right turn. Since I was aware of what lay ahead, God's miracle seemed to me to be our impending doom. My passenger, though, knew literally nothing about the future of that highway, so she naively continued in her singing and praising God for His protection—completely oblivious to the impending dangers just ahead!

God wasn't through with us that night. As we neared Tullarosa and the road signs indicated reductions of speed from 55 to 45 to 35 and finally to 20 at the turn through town, the car would slow to that exact speed, enabling us to silently and effortlessly negotiate the turn and head on through town. We passed the little church where I had intended to "abandon" the car and kept on moving. At the edge of town right beneath the sign announcing our departure from Tullarosa, our car quit—never to run again

until Monday morning when my husband and I returned to retrieve it from the desert.

The last worker from the retreat passed us almost simultaneously with our stop and took us home. All the way home, we couldn't stop talking about what had happened, and although this man was a God-fearing man, our praises and explanations seemed to fall on deaf ears. At one point my passenger turned to me jokingly, and asked, "Kathy, why didn't we just ask God to take us all the way to El Paso?"

That event happened several years ago now, but the lessons God taught me that night have returned to me again and again in recent years as I have endeavored to trust God in impossible situations. Our God is indeed a God of miracles, but as long as we have things in control, we really don't need Him or the supernatural. It is when we are at our ultimate human extremities that God can step in and work a miracle. And work miracles He does! He works miracles in all areas of our lives, whether physical, spiritual, or emotional. But when He does, the whole world will know that it was only God who could have evoked these results. He is the miracle worker, and He and He alone gets the praise and glory!

> *It is when we are at our ultimate human extremities that God can step in and work a miracle.*

The Children of Israel were like my friend and I that night on the desert when God told Moses to go to Pharoah

and plead to *"let my people go."* They had been slaves in Egypt for 430 years. It all started with the jealously of the ten older brothers of Joseph who sold him into slavery. Things went pretty well for the Hebrews after Joseph was finally venerated, but as the generations came and went, the new leaders knew little to nothing about Joseph, his brothers, and how all these aliens got to Egypt. All they knew was that the Children of Israel afforded them cheap labor, and that these aliens worshipped "A" singular God.

The Egyptians didn't even begin to comprehend the divine power wrapped up in this motley crew of foreigners. God had raised up Moses, allowed him to go to the backside of the desert for forty years because of his killing an Egyptian, and now it was God's time for a miracle. Just as God used my friend's prayer that night on the desert, God used Moses as He appealed to Pharoah ten different times. In *Exodus 3:7-8* the Lord God Jehovah speaks directly to his people through Moses: *"I have indeed seen the misery of my people in Egypt; I have heard them crying out because of their slave drivers, and I am concerned about their suffering. So, I have come down to rescue them from the hand of the Egyptians and to bring them out of that land..."*

Those of us who have read and studied these lessons and stories all our lives are limited in our imagination about the impact of the ten plagues. Try to imagine for a moment that you have never heard this story. Pharaoh hadn't heard it. The Egyptians hadn't heard it. The Children of Israel hadn't heard it. And most importantly, Moses hadn't heard it! It was new to all of them and unfolded like a great epoch before their eyes. Each plague brought a mounting sense

of impending jeopardy. The status quo was continually changing, causing both the Children of Israel and the Egyptians to feel quite insecure.

And so the plagues began to march relentlessly through the lives of the Hebrews and the Egyptians alike. To the Hebrews, the plagues were deliverance, but to the Egyptians, they would be total destruction. As twentieth century American readers, we must attempt to imagine what it was like. The plagues began with blood and frogs, both of which the magicians of Egypt were able to imitate.

Can you imagine? Can you mentally fathom what all the water being turned to blood would mean in your life? Get up to take a shower—no water, just blood! Your morning coffee is blood! Try to water you lawn—no water, just blood! When we truly get a mental handle on even the first two plagues, we would think that Pharoah would have capitulated right then. He did—temporarily! Pharoah thought he had too much to lose if the Hebrews left Egypt, and each time the immediate peril had passed, he changed his mind and hardened his heart.

But Moses was persistent. And God was consistent! And so the plagues advanced over a period of time. They just kept coming like one wave of heavy artillery after another in a military parade:

Blood! No water for a morning shower; just blood. No coffee before work; just blood. No washing clothes; just blood in the plumbing.

Frogs! Everywhere you step jumping green critters. Squealing and crunching as they are stepped on. At first little boys think this is fun, but later everyone wonders if these amphibians will ever be gone.

Gnats! Tiny little pesky bugs in your teeth, your hair, your food. Choking, swatting, constant irritants.

Flies! Pestering swarms up the nostrils of the livestock, in the windowsills, pushing in through doorway cracks. Constant fanning that never halts the circling swarms.

Anthrax! Livestock keeling over dead and stiff. Unbearable stench of rotting flesh and warnings of disease infestations.

Boils! Open, oozing, aching sores on all living things. No relief from the constant pain; no comfortable positions to be found. Continual begging for anything that would relieve the suffering.

Hail! Crops beaten into the ground; roofs damaged; demolished chariots and work carts. No one can venture from his or her home for days for fear of personal injury from large chunks of falling ice.

Locust! Black, buzzing, swirling clouds that appear in the distance, and by the time they have passed have left a corridor of devastation in their wake. The last vestige of this year's crop after the hail damage is entirely gone.

Darkness! Unfathomable, inky blackness. Sure-footed animals stumble; people make a run on lamp oil. Depression settles in. Will the sun ever rise again in the East?

Each plague was more perilous than the preceding one, and as the plagues continued one on the heels of the last, great trepidation must have built in the minds and hearts of the Egyptians. How much more of this can we withstand? Let's make it more difficult for these Hebrews. We'll double their quotas and make these ungrateful Hebrews gather their own straw for bricks. God just kept telling Moses what to do, and Moses kept following God's bidding.

And finally, God had had enough!

In some ways the Egyptians had gotten accustomed to this harassment; they were like a besieged city in the time of war. Each time a plague came and passed, they hunkered down and prepared for whatever would come next, but each time with a determination that they would be vigilant and teach these Hebrews a lesson. They would not be defeated. What they could never understand in their pagan minds, though, is that the God of Abraham, Isaac,

> *They could never understand... that the God of Abraham, Isaac, Jacob, and now the God of Moses will never be defeated!*

Jacob, and now the God of Moses will *never* be defeated!

At last, a night came that would forever change the course of human history. To the Egyptians it was just

another night, but the Hebrews knew that this night was different. Moses told the Israelites to sacrifice their purest animal and paint some of its blood over the door. What in the world for? The Hebrews had never done this before; it didn't make sense.

But God had finally gotten their undivided attention, and at this point they had total confidence in the leadership of Moses. So the Hebrews did what Moses instructed, and then they went to bed. While they were peacefully sleeping, and the Egyptians were unsuspectedly sleeping, the Angel of Death passed through Egypt.

The Egyptians had not anticipated anything like this. At last, God had gotten their attention, and when you mess with peoples' kids, you *always* get their attention! That next morning every Egyptian parent who tried to awaken his first born son was himself awakened by an incomprehensible shock. The boys who had played and laughed and accompanied their fathers emulating their every move were all gone. The son of the lowest palace worker who was learning his father's trade was gone, and the crown prince studying to some day wield the

*When you mess with peoples' kids, you **always** get their attention!*

royal scepter was gone. The benefactors who were to inherit all Egypt's wealth were dead, and with them passed the future of a once great nation.

Even the oldest Egyptian male animals were gone. They were *all* gone! During one nightmarish night of grief and

agony that forever will be canoned in world history, Egypt's future was obliterated! In the Egyptian community there was such grief and mourning that weeping and crying could be heard echoing for miles around.

On the "other side of the tracks," in the Hebrew slave camp, the story was diversely different. The Bible says that not even a dog was barking! What a contrast! What made the difference? The blood!

That sacrificial blood smeared over the door posts so many hundreds of years ago in Egypt still flows today. It flows all the way from Egypt through the Old Testament, to John the Baptist, to an old rugged cross on a hill called Calvary, to the martyrs who followed, and into our hearts and out again through our lives! The blood is the one continual flow that passes through the Word and into our daily lives; it is a crimson thread that unites us all at His feet.

It was the blood that spared the lives of the Hebrew boys. It wasn't anything they did. It wasn't whose sons they were. The Israelites didn't buy the blood, and they hadn't earned it; the blood was spilled blood from a living sacrifice, sacrificed so that they might live!

What can wash away my sin?
Nothing but the blood of Jesus!
What can make me whole again?
Nothing but the blood of Jesus!
Oh, precious is the flow
That makes me white as snow.
No other fount I know.
Nothing but the blood of Jesus!

Our God is still the God of miracles for you and me today. He wasn't just for the Egyptians in their bondage; He is for you in your bondage! He can make a stalled car run without power; He can transform an alcoholic into a family man; He can bring healing to the sick; He can bring peace to the disturbed. He wasn't just for my passenger and me one dark night on the desert in our peril and danger; He is your protector from the perils and dangers in your life. He can give you passage through any peril life may bring!

Has your life stalled out? Are you stranded? Do you feel that you have exhausted your knowledge and resources? Then, you are ready for a miracle! Our God is still the God of miracles, and the blood will never lose its power!

Chapter 2
Stuck in Winnemucca

If my husband of thirty-five years and I had had to measure the future success of our marriage on our first couple weeks together, we would have surely quit before we ever really got started! We met and married in a small college town in Southern Idaho. Since most of our mutual friends were there, we arranged our wedding plans to be the last day of the fall semester in that same little town right before the Christmas holiday break.

During the summer before our wedding, I had made all the plans, addressed invitations, ordered cake and flowers, and reserved the church so that when the fall semester began, both of us could concentrate on the job of school. We married during my senior year and my husband's junior year, and since I was an education major, that semester was the one in which I did my student teaching. Our early wedding preparations made for smooth sailing through the semester toward our wedding day.

The wedding itself went without a hitch. Although it was a cold December night outside, it was warm in the church and in our hearts. We were off (so we thought) to a great start together! Both of our families had driven from distant states—my husband's family from Washington, and mine from California. We had planned our wedding to the last detail, and it went beautifully. As soon as the reception was over, though, all chaos broke loose!

The spring before we married, my future husband and I had purchased an old '54 Chevy which I had driven to work that summer in California. During our wedding we had that old car discretely stored in a friend's garage with plans for David's best man to get us there safely and without incident. That was not to happen as smoothly as we had planned! Some of our "friends" had gotten to our best man's car, and it had four flat tires.

My father-in-law had driven from Washington that day in their old family station wagon, and he quickly handed his keys over to David for our "getaway." My father-in-law lived on the edge, and this trip was no different than any other. His car ran about one-half block before it ran out of gas.

> *There we were, newly married, being chased by an entire college population and NO available transportation.*

There we were, newly married, being chased by an entire college population and NO available transportation.

At that moment, my seventeen-year-old brother drove up in my parents' brand new '64 Chevrolet Super Sport—with four-on-the floor! He was the unacclaimed hero of the day! My new husband's instructions were short and to-the-point: *"Lose them!"* With that injunction, my young brother set out to do that very thing—lose our pursuers. This was a small town with few stop lights. However, my husband gave Steve those instructions just as he approached one of the few lights, and in Steve's youthful zeal, he promptly proceeded through a red light. David's next instructions were even more explicit: *"Step on it!"*

Fortunately, Steve did step on it, but not before a drunk driver struck us on the left rear fender. The car whirled around in the street a couple times before it finally came to rest about a half block from the light. Unbelievably, none of us were hurt although we would have most certainly have been broadsided if my husband hadn't spoken when he did. The condition of the car, though, was a different story. At least three of the tires were flat, and the driver's side was pretty "bunged up;" the door wouldn't open, the rear view mirror was missing, etc.

There we stood—married less than two hours—in the middle of the street in our best clothes, noticeably shaken, with nine-tenths of a small college town's students circled around us and my parents' damaged car. Through the haze of the moment, one of David's friends came to our rescue and transported us in his dirty old Ford to the little garage where we had our beat-up '54 Chevy stored. What a way to begin our life together! What we were not aware of that night was that this car wreck was just the beginning to the wackiest two weeks of our married life!

We went on to Boise and then to Sun Valley for a two day honeymoon. On our first day together, after we were informed that the kitchen was down and that we would not be receiving the honeymooner's breakfast we had been promised, we received a phone call—from my mother! I'll never forget the look of future foreboding on my husband's face as he held his hand over the phone mouthpiece and said, "It's your mother!" She was just calling to ease our minds about the wreck and to tell us that they were able to get the car operating enough to head back to California. Regardless, it seemed to be a bad omen of things to come.

After a couple blissful, but cold days in Sun Valley, we returned to our little rented two-room cottage down the alley from the college. Our plans were to work for a couple weeks before we drove to California for Christmas. On the evening of December 23, after my husband finished his shift at JC Penney, we set out in our '54 Chevy to drive to Sacramento.

This was not a road that was unfamiliar to us since we had traversed it several times during our dating years. We would drive through Southern Idaho, passing through a little town called Jordan Valley, then over many desolate Nevada miles to Winnemucca, and finally to Reno. From Reno, we would cross the Donner Pass and sail on into Sacramento. This entire trip usually took about twelve hours. We were young and totally unapprehensive whatsoever about arriving in Sacramento by mid-morning on December 24.

We were happy as larks as we drove along, pontificating about our future life together and this our "first" Christmas. Just on the west side of Jordan Valley, and a long way from Winnemucca, our clutch slipped and finally went out totally. My husband paid a stranger $5.00 to follow us to Winnemucca, forced the clutch into third, and I physically held the car in gear as we drove the lengthy distance to Winnemucca.

It was nearly midnight when we reached an all night truck stop/restaurant in Winnemucca. Miraculously, David was able to get a mechanic to work on the clutch, and he worked all night long in the cold while we sat "patiently" in the restaurant. We watched truckers come and go, gamble and lose, cuss and swear. (We even waited on a few tables to keep from getting so bored.)

At dawn, the mechanic pronounced the car "repaired." We paid him with a personal check (for which we had no funds), and continued our journey toward Reno. By now we were both tired from lack of sleep but felt good that we had averted a total breakdown and possible disaster along the highway somewhere in the wilderness. We knew that we would be home in a few short hours. Christmas was the next day, and that this would be a great family time together as we all celebrated our new marriage and my parents' twenty-fifth wedding anniversary.

> *By now we were both tired from lack of sleep but felt good that we had averted a total breakdown and possible disaster...*

Our exuberance was short-lived, though, for less than fifty miles west of Winnemucca, the "repaired" clutch went out. Again, David forced the clutch into third gear, and after several more hours, we limped into Reno, knowing full-well that there was no way this car would be finishing the trip to Sacramento in time for Christmas.

It was now early on Christmas Eve, and there wasn't a single garage open. Finally, we found a mechanic at a gas station who agreed to keep our car and fix it a couple days *after* Christmas! We were stranded, tired, and broke! Throughout this "journey" we had been calling my parents with periodic updates, and sometime during this ordeal we coined the infamous expression— "Stuck in Winnemucca."

Once again we called them with the latest "disaster" report. Mutually, we agreed that they would send my older brother (an experienced driver) over the Donner Pass in the newly repaired Chevy Super Sport. Having no money for a motel and little for food, we simply waited several more hours in a Denney's restaurant for my brother to arrive. It was late on Christmas Eve, and I'm sure we were a pitiful sight.

Sometime in the wee hours of Christmas morning, my brother arrived at the Denney's restaurant. A "happy camper" was not a term that applied to him that cold, wintry night. Together we grabbed a quick bite to eat and began our trip across Donner Pass in the biggest snowstorm of the season. We were determined to get across that pass before the road was closed and we had to spend what was left of our first Christmas together stranded in the snow with my older brother.

The snow was blinding, and my husband had a sick headache. While he laid in the back seat, I tried to navigate for my brother. There were times when we actually could not see the road, but we kept plowing on and finally came down the pass into Truckee and at last to Sacramento. Christmas was nearly over when we arrived, but the family had saved the Christmas tree for us to share.

When we finally got rested from the long journey, the remainder of our time in Sacramento was tremendous. We were given a big reception by friends, were able to spend some time in San Francisco, and generally had a great time. All this time, though, there was the nagging realization that sooner or later we had to face the situation of our abandoned car in Reno.

We were to leave Sacramento with my foster brother and his wife who were home for Christmas and would be returning to Minnesota December 30. They would take us as far as Reno and our car. In theory this sounded smooth, but nothing on this entire trip had gone as planned, and our "luck" continued.

> *In theory this sounded smooth, but nothing on this entire trip had gone as planned, and our "luck" continued.*

December 30 that year Donner Pass was hit with yet another huge snowstorm and was temporarily closed. We watched television all day, hoping that they would clear the pass enough that the four of us could leave. Around 4:00 PM an announcement was made that the roads were

cleared for travel but might not stay open long. We decided to give the pass a try and set off in their station wagon— the four of us with Molly, their cocker spaniel.

The pass was rough, and the storm severe, but we were able to get behind a snowplow and make it into Reno before the pass was closed again. We picked up our repaired car, paid for the new clutch with another personal check (with no funds to cover it). All four of us were exhausted, so somewhere in the middle of nowhere in Nevada, we found a little motel and rented two cheap rooms for a few hours of sleep.

My foster brother and his wife agreed to follow us as far as Winnemucca so that together, he and my husband could get our first check back from the mechanic who had "repaired" our car Christmas Eve. It was already December 31 when we got to Winnemucca and completed this transaction. Consequently, my brother and his wife decided to follow us all the way to our little house in Southern Idaho and return to Minnesota from there.

Not far east of Winnemucca in the Nevada desert where the speed limit was actually posted "reasonable and proper," and where you could drive nearly a hundred miles without a bend in the road or without seeing another vehicle, our old car began to make a deafening racket. Simultaneous to this noise and like a mirage from nowhere, there appeared a desolate looking old house down a long dirt road near the highway.

Our little caravan turned in there—once again totally at the mercy of strangers. An old fellow came out of a dilapidated house, walked up to our car, and announced,

"Young man, your car needs a rocker arm." I had never heard of a rocker arm, but this angel of a man had a collection of old wrecked cars by the side of his house, and in that mess found a rocker arm, repaired our car, refused payment, and again we were on our way. To this day, I'm certain if that old fellow was actually there, or if he was an angel God sent to rescue us. Whichever way, to us it was a miracle!

We were still driving in tandem with my foster brother and his wife, and by now it was late on December 31. We soon found ourselves in yet another snowstorm. The only thing we could do was stop for the night, and the only place to stop was the little town of Jordan Valley. To our chagrin as newlyweds, the four of us could find only *one* available motel room in the entire town! So, we rented it! Four adults and one dog in one motel room, and two of us married just barely two weeks. The crowning discovery for us, though, was our discovery that December 31 was my foster brother and wife's fifth wedding anniversary!

So... David and I took one incredibly long walk in the snow. We found a gas station that was open, purchased the anniversary couple a little glob of a chocolate candy bar called a *Mountain Bar*, then knocked on several doors in town until we found someone who would give us five birthday candles. When we got back to the hotel room, they were already in bed. David and I went into the bathroom, lit the candles, and came out singing, *"Happy Anniversary to You."* Pretty young and dumb! But a great memory! Finally, the next day we limped back into Idaho and our little cottage down the alley.

What a two weeks! After this bumpy start, David and I felt that together we could tackle and conquer any situation that life could dish out. For thirty-five plus years now that two weeks, and especially that incredible trip to California, has been a hallmark for us. It has been a point-of-reference for my entire family. Whenever *anyone* is in trouble of *any* kind all he or she has to say is: "I'm *STUCK IN WINNEMUCCA*. That immediately alerts the other family members that that person is in need of help, that they are desperate, and that the situation is critical.

> *Whenever anyone is in trouble of any kind all he or she has to say is: "I'm STUCK IN WINNEMUCCA."*

The Children of Israel were in a similar situation to ours when they wandered in the desert of the Sinai Peninsula. Just as my husband and I were *STUCK IN WINNEMUCCA,* the Children of Israel were *STUCK IN THE SINAI.* Just like my husband and I in those first couple weeks of marriage, nothing was working, and things seemed to going from bad to worse.

Like our goal for a good marriage was admirable, the Children of Israel had a good goal—the Promised Land. But similar to us in our journey to California, they seemed to be making no headway. In fact, for a large portion of their forty years of wandering, they were digressing from God's appointed instructions. Chapters three and four of Joshua relate this story of the Children of Israel. The Children of Israel were indeed *STUCK IN THE SINAI!*

Since the days of Moses, the Children of Israel had wandered in the desert forty years. That was not God's plan. Rather, it was man's alteration of the plan when God's people failed to listen to Joshua and Caleb forty years earlier. The Children of Israel were intimidated by the mundane forces of the earth and saw ordinary people as giants and themselves as grasshoppers. They failed to attain the glory, excitement, and jubilation of God's initial deliverance.

God had every intention of sending His people directly to the Promised Land after they crossed the Red Sea and left Egypt. Their hesitation—conceived by a negative majority report and nurtured by a negative people—caused the Children of Israel to have to endure forty years of desolation and emptiness that were never intended by God.

After forty years, God was ready to permit the Children of Israel to move on—to move on to the land of milk and honey where the "grapes of Eshcol grow" that He had promised them forty years earlier. This was the same land that He had full intentions of them possessing under Moses' leadership—*God's Promised Land!*

Just as God had vowed when the Children of Israel failed to believe Joshua and Caleb, God had allowed an entire generation to perish in the desert. They had wandered and roamed, fussed and complained, until the last negative reporter gone. Even in ancient days, this journey should not have taken more than a couple weeks, but now after *forty* years, it was time to move. Can you get a handle on that? Forty years! That's two entire generations. It's not a delay of a season, or even a year. It's *forty years!*

But, when God says it is time, **it's time!**

Now, after forty years, God has set the scene for one *ordinary day to become an extraordinary day.* He is ready to do what He had promised years earlier. God is set to reorder forever the lives of the Israelites in one fell swoop! There are going to be some major changes in their lives, and those changes are going to be totally at God's direction.

Chapter 3
An "Extraordinary" Ordinary Day

One "extraordinary" ordinary day, Joshua—the very same Joshua who tried to inspire the Children of Israel to proceed to the Promised Land forty years earlier—announced, *"Consecrate yourselves, for tomorrow the Lord will do amazing things among you,"* *(Joshua 3:3)*. To the Children of Israel, this day was no different than the past 14,600 days. It was just another day to dismantle the tents, aimlessly walk a few miles, and then re-pitch the tents for yet another pointless night in one more nameless location.

But, God had another plan for that "extraordinary" ordinary day. God Almighty was returning to His original Plan "A" that He had intended to fulfill forty years earlier. His initial plan was just as viable this "extraordinary" ordinary day as it had been forty years previously. Now, though, the Children of Israel had a mind to trust their leader, Joshua, and to believe that God could actually do what He had said He would do!

Joshua continued in his declaration of determination and immediacy as he instructed the priests, *"Take up the ark of the covenant and pass on ahead of the people. So, they took it up and went ahead of them,"* *(Joshua 3:6).* Go back and research this passage if you will. There is NO reference of discussion or argument with Joshua by the priests. They simply and obediently did what he commanded. God was moving in their hearts as well as in the heart of Joshua, their leader. They didn't know what was forthcoming, but they had an innate sense that God was at work!

> **They didn't know what was forthcoming, but they had an innate sense that God was at work!**

Joshua captured the people's undivided, undistracted attention this "extraordinary" ordinary day as he gathered them around himself on the banks of the Jordan River: *"Come and listen to the words of the Lord your God. This is how you will know that the living God is among you and that He will certainly drive out before you the Canaanites, Hittites, Hivites, and the 'excetorites',"* *(Joshua 3:9-10).*

Joshua's instructions (given him by God) were simple: The priests were to carry the Ark of the Covenant into the Jordan River, and when the first priest of the twelve set his little toe in the river, it would be begin to roll back and "stack up." Joshua had never seen the Jordan River roll back. The priests had never seen it. And the people surely had never seen it! Collectively, however, they ALL believed! Joshua gave God's commands, the priests obeyed,

and the people followed. It was as simple, and yet as complex, as that. A clear, intelligible, understandable, simple formula: *"Trust and obey, for there's no other way."* Forty years had proven that; there was indeed no other way but to trust the Lord!

Let your imagination take a journey with these people this "extraordinary" ordinary day. When they began to see the Jordan (which was then at flood stage) roll back and "stack up," a wave of disbelief and then a surge of acceptance must have rolled through this congregation. They had been *"STUCK IN THE SINAI"* for forty years. The Israelites had become accustomed to their nomadic, pointless existence. They might have remembered, but their memories were only a dull recollection that *they* were the Children of Israel, His select few! Like the old spiritual declares, *"They'd been down so long, gettin' up hadn't crossed their minds!"*

Slowly a corporate awareness of who they really were, who their God really was, and what their God was capable of performing began to course and pulsate and accelerate through these people. God had not forgotten them. Their forty years of wanderings were OVER! Salvation and deliverance were visible and audible as they saw and heard the mighty Jordan River roll back and "stack up."

Acceptance of reality was slow at first but quickened with an unbelievable rapidity as person by person the Children of Israel began to gingerly step onto the dry river bottom. Then, there must have been an avalanche effect that coursed through the company as they began to race en masse, shouting and praising God, nearly trampling one

another as they stampeded into the dry river. And in the center of all this excitement and festivity were the priests: *"The priests who carried the Ark of the Covenant of the Lord stood firm on dry ground in the middle of the Jordan, while all Israel passed by until the whole nation had completed the crossing on dry ground," (Joshua 3:17).*

Can you see it? Are you able to get a mental handle on what was occurring? As thousands of Israelites, their families, flocks, and possessions crossed *through* the river on dry ground, twelve priests were standing in the middle of them on the dry river bed holding the Ark of the Covenant above their heads. There wasn't a single man, woman, child, or animal that day that did not pass the priests and the ark.

As each Israelite passed the ark, he or she was reminded of God's constant and continual protection during forty miserable years. God remained central with the ark. The ark kept the Children of Israel focused in the knowledge that it was God who had parted these waters. This was not some freak act of nature or some deed of heathen sorcery. This was an unexplainable miracle from God, and it was being coupled in its very epicenter by the Ark of the Covenant.

> **This was not some freak act of nature or some deed of heathen sorcery, this was an unexplainable miracle from God...**

This was the same ark that the Children of Israel had guarded and protected through forty years of wandering; the same ark that held Moses' rod, the same ark that held

the Ten Commandments; the same ark that contained a "serving" of the manna from heaven; the same ark that would one day embrace its promised site in the *Holy of Holies* in Jerusalem's Temple; the same ark that the Children of Israel trusted as a symbol of God's protection and provision.

This was not a substitute ark used just in case the river rolled back to flood stage. It was authentic and genuine—no substitutions! If this miracle failed and the waters rolled back to flood stage, the ark and the priests all would go down together to their deaths. There must have been absolute compliance and trust among the Children of Israel that "extraordinary" ordinary day. There is no human explanation why a people who had allowed themselves to roam aimlessly forty years, circling and re-circling the same territory repeatedly, would on this particular day *"trust and obey."*

The climax of the celebration was yet to come! In Joshua Chapter 4, God instructs Joshua to send twelve men (one from each tribe) to return to the dry river bed while the twelve priests were still standing on it, holding up the ark. These men were just ordinary members from each tribe—no one particularly special or select—just one representative from each tribe. These tribal representatives were to each choose one stone and retrieve it from the dry river bottom.

What an honor it must have been for these twelve men to do this seemingly meaningless task! Perhaps each man searched the river's bottom to find a unique rock—one that would be identifiable from the other eleven as his tribe's

rock so that future generations could point to the specific rock from their tribe, and say, *"That's our rock!"*

These twelve stones were to be large; we know this because the Bible instructs that they must be carried out of the riverbed on the men's shoulders (Joshua 4:5). Individually, these stones were to be a lasting memorial to the Children of Israel of God's miracle in the parting of the Jordan (Joshua 4:6). Collectively, though, these stones had a much higher significance than just being rocks taken from the dry bottom of the Jordan River. God had a plan—a plan that would provide a means for the Children of Israel to remember this "extraordinary," ordinary day forever!

On the tenth day after the crossing of the Jordan, Joshua instructed the Children of Israel to camp at a place called Gilgal. At that holy spot, Joshua set up the twelve stones—one from each of the tribes—taken from the dry river bottom of the Jordan, forming an altar. Then Joshua addressed the people: *"In the future when your children ask you why these stones are in this place and what do these stones mean? Tell them 'Israel crossed the Jordan here on dry ground, and God worked a miracle in this place'"* (Joshua 4:21).

> **Do you get it? This is shouting ground!**

Do you get it? This is shouting ground! If Joshua had anything to say about it, never again would children be allowed to suffer because of parents' reluctance to follow God's leadership. This altar would be a marker—a collective, corporate marker of God's miraculous deliverance. There is such an enormous lesson here that

it's hard for us to get our "spiritual hands" around it. Through our own hesitation or through circumstances that are beyond our control or through a combination of both of these, we often find ourselves mired, wandering, confused, and *STUCK IN WINNEMUCCA!*

We wander and grope and reach and hesitate until (as my old West Texas aunt says) we are *"flat wore out."* Either through His word or through one of His earthly leaders, God comes to us on an "extraordinary" ordinary day and says: *"Follow me. I want you to step out in faith and just put your toe in the river."*

"Put my toe in the river! That's silly and doesn't make sense. I would be embarrassed for my friends to see me do something that inane." When that is our response, there is nothing God can do with us but let us continue to wander and roam. But when our response is, "God, I don't get it, but if you say for me to do it, there must be a reason," then He's able to work a miracle—a miracle that only He could do.

The miracle is not complete, however, until we acknowledge it and build an altar. Our kids and family and friends MUST know! We must mark the spot where God allowed us to turn a miraculous corner in our trust and obedience. These markers (or altars) become continual reminders to present and future generations that in spite of our human hesitations and weaknesses, God has worked miracles in the past and will continue to do so in the future.

Under Joshua's leadership, the Children of Israel did what my husband and I did on our trip through Winnemucca. In the future when you are confronted with

an impossible situation, remember to keep persevering, get the broken fixed, leave behind what isn't working, go on with life, enjoy the adventure, and when the miracle comes, build an altar as a testimony to your children, family, and friends that your God is still the God of miracles and the impossible situation.

Ten summers ago our life as a family was challenged beyond our wildest imagination. My husband was without work and finishing his doctorate; I was finishing my master's degree; we had one child in college and the other ready to enter college in the fall. We had thought that a job would be forthcoming for my husband before the summer was over, but that job came all too slowly.

In front of the kids, David and I tried to keep an optimistic facade, but privately we were getting desperate and wondering where God was in this entire process. We were able to keep afloat for several months by living on credit, postponing car payments, and cashing in insurance policies, but a day of reckoning was fast approaching. During the summer, we had been able to maintain all of our mortgage payments but that could not continue when school began and we had two students in college! We were desperate!

One Sunday that summer in late July my husband was invited to the Seattle area to be a guest speaker at a small church. On our way home, driving down I-5 that Sunday evening as we drove and talked, we both felt strangely moved that we should stop somewhere and once again pray and beseech the Lord on behalf of our family and our present situation. Both of us knew of a brand new church located

in Olympia along the interstate and decided that we would stop there, go in, and pray together. To our disappointment, though, church was over when we got there. Everyone was gone, and the building was locked tighter than a drum. Just one more obstacle—it seemed to us—in a baffling summer.

As we turned to get back into our car and leave the church parking lot, we were both taken by a pile of rocks in front of this beautiful new building. Why was a pile of rocks in front of a beautiful, new modern structure? As David and I inspected that pile of rocks we discovered a bronze plaque with this inscription: *"Joshua 4:21."* In one joint motion, my husband and I ran to the car to get a Bible, and there we read the words Joshua had given to the Children of Israel after that "extraordinary" ordinary day: *"In the future when your children ask you why these rocks are here, tell them God worked a miracle in this place."*

That pile of rocks became our altar that quiet, warm Northwest summer evening as once again we reminded God of our situation—which He knew all about in the first place. When we arrived home that night, my husband and I sat down with both of our children on the edge of our son's waterbed and told them about our encounter. As they looked at us in bewilderment, we told them that we didn't know how, but we *knew* that God had an imminent answer for our

> *That pile of rocks became our altar that quiet, warm Northwest summer evening.*

dilemma, that we weren't going to lose our home, that Dad would be getting employment soon, and that we would be

able to send them both back to college if that is what they wanted.

Now, we had to step out by faith into our own flooding Jordan, not knowing what or how God would deal with us and our situation— but confidant that our God—the same God of Joshua—was in control!

> *Now, we had to step out by faith into our own flooding Jordan...*

Within two weeks my husband was offered a position as a university professor that offered both of our children tuition remission at the Christian college of their choice. From out of the blue I was offered temporary work for the rest of the summer. And finally, one "extraordinary," ordinary day while we were packing a van to leave our home of seven years and had no buyer for that home, the Lord literally sent a man into our lives who moved into our house the day we moved out and rented it for the following year. Now that is, indeed, a "God thing."

Do any of the four of us aspire to relive that summer? **NO, and again I say NO!** But, the lessons we learned that summer remain with us all. Are we thankful that we put our foot into the Jordan that summer, Sunday evening? **YES, and again I say YES!**

"I do not consider myself yet to have taken hold of it. But one thing I do: Forgetting what is behind and straining toward what is ahead, I press on toward the goal to win the prize for which God has called me heavenward in Christ Jesus" (Philippians 3:13).

Chapter 4
The Little Red Dog House

Our daughter was one of those lively children—the kind who never sit or stand still. She was a charmer, though, and never hurt anyone. She was just active! Since I have taught school for years, I was familiar with all the labels—ADD, ADHD, hyperactive, etc. She could have easily fit two or three of those labels, and while she was growing up, I was always cognizant that there was a raft of doctors out there who would happily medicate her. For fleeting moments from time to time I was tempted to let some doctor have a field day with her, but those temptations were always only fleeting.

If you have ever been around an active child, you would recognize Dana. She was always on the move—jumping, skipping, running, dancing, and basically enjoying childhood. I remember watching her stand on her head upside down in a chair with her legs over the back of that chair watching TV

backwards through her legs. How her brain was able to process this is still one of life's deepest mysteries.

Anyone with less that two weeks' parenting experience knows that when a child like Dana is quiet, trouble is brewing. Such a day occurred sometime during her first grade year. While I was cooking dinner, I began to notice that she was going back and forth through the kitchen and out into the garage. At first it was no big deal, but as she began her third or fourth trip into the house, I could sense some frustration and agitation coming from her little psyche.

Several more of these trips ensued, and with each trip into the house, I could see that she was getting quieter and more frustrated. Being the wise mother that I always was, I decided to lay down my dinner preparations and go to the garage for myself to see what was going on. There, I was greeted by an overwhelming sight!

Ever since our son was one year old, our family has always had a dog. We are *dog people!* Consequently, we had a dog when Dana was born, and the entire time we were raising children, we had dogs. We were all attached to Mrs. Beasley, our small little terrier that stood only a foot or so high. She had black fir and a big fluffy tail that curled up over her back. She was sweet and lovable and predated Dana by a year and a half.

In the garage that day Dana was endeavoring to construct a doghouse for Mrs. Beasley. She had a stack of lumber that we had picked up for our fireplace from a construction site near by, and beside that pile of lumber

she had two three-by-five cards. On these cards she had drawn a schematic of her six-year-old version of a doghouse—a side view and a frontal view. Both of the drawings were pretty good and actually resembled a doghouse. There were some vital missing elements, however.

To begin with Dana had no hammer and no nails—virtually no tools—just a plan. I watched her. She would study her little plan on her three-by-five cards and then carefully attempt to stack the lumber in the semblance of her schematic. But it just wasn't working! And a little spirited, brown-eyed six-year-old was getting more and more frustrated.

My mother's heart was touched! There weren't many incidents in my child-rearing days in which I felt inspired, but this must have been one of the few. I knew, you see, that just across the inter- national border from El Paso in Juarez, Mexico that darling little doghouses could be purchased for virtually NO money.

> *There weren't many incidents in my child-rearing days in which I felt inspired, but this must have been one of the few.*

I spoke to my child and said, "Dana, if you can lay your plans aside and wait until your daddy gets home from work, he knows a place where you can get a doghouse even more suitable for Mrs. Beasley than the one you have drawn—one already completely finished."

She looked at me in bewilderment and disbelief. How could this be possible? She had worked so hard with no results, and now I was telling her that doghouses were available just for the asking. How incredulous! Her question to me was a mature and practical one for any age and especially for a six-year-old: "How much does a doghouse cost?"

My stroke of wisdom continued as I returned the question, "How much do you have?"

As quick as her little active legs would carry her, she was off to her bedroom to count her funds and gather her resources. Just as quickly as she left, Dana was back in the kitchen with her own personal financial report and the announcement that she had $2.67.

"Dana," I responded, "that's exactly how much a doghouse costs—you have just exactly enough—$2.67! If you can wait until tomorrow, your dad knows exactly where to go for you to purchase a doghouse. Tomorrow morning the four of us will go together, and you can select just the perfect doghouse for Mrs. Beasley and pay for it with your own money." She didn't fully understand, but she trusted her father and me, so she agreed and waited.

Her waiting wasn't patient, though, for she was anxious to get on with her plan. When my husband arrived home from work that day, she went flying to him to announce that mother said he knew where to get a doghouse for Mrs. Beasley. A rather confused husband greeted me in the kitchen that night, but after my explanation, he comprehended the significance of this venture. It was

mutually agreed that tomorrow—Saturday—we would head across the border to Juarez in search of a doghouse.

That was no ordinary Saturday morning at our house, for two very enthusiastic children were jumping up and down on our bed early in the morning urging us out and on to get the doghouse. Together, the four of us set out on Dana's international adventure. Once in Juarez, it didn't take us long to locate the ideal doghouse for Mrs. Beasley. Dana selected a little house with a shingled roof and an

> *Her little six-year-old mind just couldn't comprehend how her dad knew exactly where to go to purchase such a*

arched door. It met and even superceded all her specification. It was perfect! Her little six-year-old mind just couldn't comprehend how her dad knew exactly where to go to purchase such a treasure. I'm not exactly sure what the final cost of that doghouse was that day, but as far as Dana knew, it cost $2.67.

We put the doghouse in the trunk, tied it down, and headed back to our home across the border in the United States. Just before we got home, we stopped at a hardware store, and our son rather begrudgingly (being of a different temperament) parted with $1.42 of his money and purchased a small can of red paint.

When we reached our home, the children put the doghouse in the backyard, and together painted it red! When that red paint dried, the two of them stood back and

presented the *little red doghouse* to our little mutt, Mrs. Beasley as though it were the Taj Majal!

What a day! Just the day before a little child's plans were "on the rocks." They were viable and possible, but she didn't have the proper tools or skills, and her plans were simply not working. But her father knew just exactly what she wanted and knew just exactly where to go to get it. She just had to be willing to sacrifice what little she had in order to fulfill her dream.

That incident was over twenty years ago, and shortly after the "doghouse episode" Mrs. Beasley was killed and she was replaced with our little schnauzer, Heidi, who was with us for seventeen years. Long ago we left El Paso, Texas and have lived and worked in several states since. Dana and her brother, Scott, are both grown and graduated from college and on their own. But the memories and lessons of those two days are still with me and with all of us, for God spoke to me through a little six-year-old that day.

Many times we are like Dana. We're inexperienced and immature and don't have the proper tools, but we have a plan. And our plan seems like a good one! We draw our little plans and head out to the garages of our lives and try to force those plans into existence, but they just don't work. And we get more and more frustrated. We try harder while we fuss and fume about our good plan that

> *We're inexperienced and immature and don't have the proper tools, but we have a plan.*

just won't work. And then our omniscient Father comes. He sees us in our dilemma, and His great heart is moved.

"Daughter/Son," He asks, "what are you trying to build?"

"I'm building a doghouse, sir. Can't you see that I have these neat plans? Can't you see that I have the lumber? Can't you see that I have willing hands? Why won't this work?"

"Daughter/Son," He continues, "do you have any other resources?"

"Nothing, sir! Nothing, but $2.67. And that isn't enough to amount to anything or even consider using for a significant purchase."

"Are you willing to relinquish that $2.67 to me and trust me with it?"

"But Father, $2.67 is all I have, and if I give it to you, I have nothing!"

"Daughter/son, do you comprehend the eternal dynamic here? Without me, you *are* nothing! *But you can do all things through me, for I strengthen you"* (Philippians 4:13).

> ***Do you comprehend the eternal dynamic here? Without me, you are nothing!***

As long as we clutch our measly human resources tightly in our spiritual fist, He allows it. Although He is a

jealous God, He is not assertive when it comes to our will. He wants us to *want* Him! God knows that there is never a true mutual love relationship until both parties want to trust the other and put the other above themselves.

He is the ultimate—the paramount—lover. God knows that if He forces Himself on us that in doing so He negates our humanity. Our humanity—our likeness to God—is what separates us from the other animals and draws us to Him! And Him to us! *"I have loved thee with an everlasting love; therefore, with loving kindness have I drawn thee"* *(Jeremiah 31:3).*

At last our finite humanness begins to comprehend it! This is God Almighty and His son Jesus endeavoring to communicate with our spirit. Not pushing. Just nudging and patiently waiting. Until little by little we begin to release our grip on our measly $2.67, let our fingers roll back and relax. And with a hesitant gesture, we offer our all to Him.

And when we relinquish control of our meager resources—our $2.67—and place it *all* in His hands, we become partners with Almighty God Himself. It is at the point when we willingly accept Him as our partner and place our puny resources at His disposal—resources that He made accessible to us in the first place—that a cosmic miracle begins to occur.

> *When we relinquish control of our meager resources—our $2.67—and place it* all *in His hands, we become partners with Almighty God Himself.*

He takes our little nothing—our $2.67—amalgamates it with His everything, and the two become indistinguishable. He and we are one! His resources become our resources, and His abundant supply of resources becomes accessible because we have finally relinquished ownership to our nothing.

He knows exactly where to go to fill our every need—and more often than not, our every want. Sometimes (as in the case of our little daughter) He takes us to a completely different country—a country where He has resources that are unfathomable to our childlike minds and spheres of existence. We stand amazed.

How could we have hoarded our $2.67 so long? It all seems so simple and understandable now. All His resources were available all the time—totally at our disposal by the Father's design. His resources always supercede our petty little schemes and plans. He doesn't push. He waits. He doesn't coerce. He waits for us to make the decision to accept His plan. What makes the difference? How is this cycle completed, and how are we guided into an amazing oneness with Him and His resources and divine provisions?

One word! **TRUST!** When we uncurl that first finger and its tenacious grip on our measly $2.67, and when we finalize the transaction by relinquishing our last hold of our own plans and extend the entire $2.67 to Him, we begin an amazing journey of trust—a journey that may take us over land and sea. A journey that may hold good times or bad times. A journey that will surely embody tears as well as celebration. But a journey that is divinely accompanied.

What a journey! No one can comprehend it or fathom its adventure until it is experienced.

When we walk with the Lord in the light of His word,
What a joy He sheds on our way.
While we do His good will, He abides with us still.
And to all who will trust and obey.
Trust and obey. For there's no other way
To be happy in Jesus but to trust and obey!

Chapter 5
The Hooterville Express

My grandmother was a remarkable woman! She lived to be 96 years old and raised three children: my mother, her sister, and her brother. What was unique about Gramma, though, was that she was widowed twice and only lived as a married woman fifteen years of her total 96. The rest of her entire adult life she either was raising her children or living alone.

Despite her setbacks she had an indomitable spirit, and I remember her as one of the most delightful individuals of my entire childhood. All my life I remember her living in a remodeled three-car garage and, up until the time she retired, working incredibly hard.

Regardless of how tired she was from her job as a maid or cook, Gramma always had time to laugh, tell her childhood adventures, go through old picture albums, or play her guitar and sing. She was a grand, old lady. As she

grew older, Gramma had two wishes that all of us heard repeatedly. She wanted to leave something tangible behind for her children, and she **DID NOT** want to be a burden on the family when she was old!

Through a series of nearly unbelievable circumstances, she was able to fulfill her first wish far beyond her wildest dreams or expectations. But sadly, her second wish never came true. She lived alone until she was 95 when the family was forced to move her to an "adult group home."

Gramma hated this place, but it just had to be. When she had been there just a few months, she suffered a massive stroke. Had she had been at home, she would have surely passed at that time. Paramedics who came to the home, however, were forced to resuscitate her, and her final months were spent in total dependency. She lost control of *everything* but her mind! There was no dignity, and she was miserable!

During this unbearably long year my mother would occasionally go from her home in southwestern Idaho to be with Gramma in southwestern Oregon to assist her sister with the care-giving. After one such trip, Mother called to say that she would be flying up to our home in Vancouver, Washington after her Medford visit to see our family, and that my dad would drive from Idaho and pick her up at our place.

Being a frequent flyer, I was aware that my mother would be flying to Portland on a small plane—a small plane that I call the *"Hooterville Express."* The kind you need to crawl on and then crawl off. The plane without a flight attendant. The kind of plane you know that you are in deep

trouble when the travel agent informs you: "Everyone gets a window seat." Scary, little planes. Every time I fly one of these planes I wonder if I've lost my last thread of sanity for taking such a wager with my future. *That's* what I call the *"Hooterville Express,"* and *that* was what my mother would be flying to Portland.

I was also aware of the constant state of construction and turmoil the Portland airport has been in for nearly a decade. Since my mother doesn't walk well due to an old injury, it seemed the proper and considerate thing to actually park the car, go to the gate, and meet her there. When I got to the gate that day, I was surprised by a large crowd. I was curious what

> *I was curious what important person or celebrity might be coming in on the "Hooterville Express..."*

important person or celebrity might be coming in on the *"Hooterville Express"* that had generated such a crowd.

While I waited for the plane, I began to scan this crowd. It was a group of about forty people, and as I studied them, it became apparent that they were an extended family. The focal point of the entire group was a young man about twenty years old. He was neatly dressed, and as he waited, he held a long stemmed red rose between his hands. He was rubbing the stem of that rose back and forth between his hands so vigorously that it was apparent that if something didn't happen soon, he might wear the stem into two pieces.

The more I studied this family, the more intrigued I became. There were people of all ages; there were video cameras; there were instamatic cameras; and most of all there was a prevailing atmosphere of excitement and anticipation. Being a curious sort, I rather gingerly moved toward this family because it seemed to me that something extraordinary was imminent. As I drew closer to this circle, I began to pick up enough conversation to ascertain what was about to occur. My supposition from what I heard was that this young man had been overseas, had married a foreign bride, and that soon she would be arriving at this very gate from some distant land.

Shortly, there was an arrival announcement, but it wasn't the *"Hooterville Express."* It was for a jumbo jet—a huge airplane—one with a lot of numbers behind its name. I've been on a few international flights, and I am well aware that one is never at his/her best when arriving from a long flight. When you've been in the air for numerous hours, your clothes are crumpled; you need to brush your teeth; your hair is in disarray; and you need a bath. Sometimes you're a little sick from motion sickness and your legs are a bit wobbly from sitting so long. You leave the plane carrying burdens of all shapes and sorts—backpacks, coats, luggage, purses, infant paraphernalia, gifts, etc. Overall, you're a mess!

When that particular transatlantic plane finally taxied to the gate and the jetway was extended, the entire family stood up *en masse* and moved toward the jetway in a "V" formation like birds in flight with the young man and his rose as the "lead bird." There was an air of excitement—so much so that I found myself toward the back of the "V"

formation moving with them as though a magnetic force were drawing me along.

Weary travelers began to disembark, and as each person exited the plane, the anticipation of the group rose. At last, a very bedraggled, disheveled young woman appeared toting all the typical traveler's gear. Boom! The anticipation crescendoed. That young man didn't see the crumpled clothes or the hair that was in disarray or the rather frightened look on her countenance.

Not at all! What he did was amazing. He simply took her in his arms, embraced her, gave her the rose, shouldered her burdens, and while time seemed to stand still for a few seconds, he just held her close in his arms. I was touched and overwhelmed. But what

> *I don't believe that I could have dreamed or imagined the scenario that unfolded before me that day.*

transpired next was even more moving. If I hadn't witnessed it with my own eyes and ears, I don't believe that I could have dreamed or imagined the scenario that unfolded before me that day.

The young man stood back, and the family moved forward. His young bride must have been totally overwhelmed. One by one these *strangers* began to embrace her. It was touching. Since I had attached myself to the group, I situated myself close enough to hear what was being said.

The first person to embrace this tired, young woman was a woman about forty-five years old. In my new position in this "V," I heard her say, "Welcome to our family. I'm your new mother!" Then I heard, "Welcome to Portland; I'm your brother Bob." "Welcome to the great Northwest; I'm your cousin, Sue." "Welcome to our family; I'm your Uncle Joe." And on and on.

All my life I've been part of a "family," and when I married, I became a part of yet another "family." I am very aware that all families—even the most healthy—have habits and customs, secrets and past events that are peculiar to that family. But *no one* that day was advising this young woman of all the ***things*** that it would be important and necessary for her to know in order to be a good family member.

I'm sure that that particular young man had someone in his family who would have loved to have filled her in on all the juicy bits of knowledge that she *needed* to know. Someone who would fill in all the gaps and get her up-to-speed! Everyone knows exactly what this means! Fortunately, his family had had the wisdom to leave that aunt home to cook the dinner! The love I felt in this airport terminal was overpowering; there was *nothing* but love!

> **The love I felt in this airport terminal was overpowering; there was nothing but love!**

No tantalizing morsels of family history that just *had* to be told; no family skeletons revealed. All that was extended to her was love and goodness. But the demonstration wasn't over!

Apparently I wasn't the only person in the Portland airport that day who was drawn into this celebration. On the opposite side of the "V" there was another woman who had been an imposter like me and had witnessed the entire "homecoming" from the other side of the "V." From out of the blue, she began to talk and walk directly through the family and toward the young woman as though she were Moses parting the Red Sea.

It seemed almost sacrilegious to me for this woman to intrude on such a private family occasion. Since it was obvious, however, that she was going to speak regardless of what I thought, and since I was already a part of the "V," I drew a little closer in order to hear what was so important that she felt it necessary to interrupt this precious "Kodak moment."

What she said nearly blew me away! "Excuse me," she began as she focused intently on the young woman, "I can't help but notice what has been happening here today." She was looking directly at the young woman as she continued, "It's very evident to me that you have married this young man and are just today arriving in the States and meeting his family. I just have to tell you," she said, "that twenty years ago I was a foreign bride arriving in the US for the first time, and *the United States of America is all the good things people say it is and a whole lot more!*"

By this time I was weeping, and I had totally missed the arrival announcement of the little plane from "Hooterville." The next thing I knew, I saw my mother limping her way across the tarmac and into the terminal.

"Kathy," she said as she saw me weeping. "I'm so glad you're glad to see me." I'm not stupid, so I just went with that for a little while, taking advantage of the moment. When my mother could see that my tears were about something other than her arrival, she said, "Kathy, what has been happening here today?" The answer to her question has been ringing and echoing in my heart ever since.

I've thought about that day and then thought about it some more. It occurs to me that what I witnessed is not unlike what the true church should be. Most of us acknowledge that we are to be witnesses, but we lack confidence that we are adequate enough to actually tell someone about Christ. In reality, it's all very simple.

Every day each one of us has a jetway backed up to our lives, and *daily* people are exiting directly *into* our lives: our co-workers, our children, gas station attendants, beauticians, neighbors, etc. They are tired and weary; they are frightened; they are alone; often they don't look like us; they don't speak our language;

> **They are tired and weary; they are frightened; they are alone...**

and many if not all of them are carrying heavy, heavy burdens. They are loaded with more than they can bear; often they are near their own personal breaking point.

Then they walk right into our lives! These travelers aren't arriving into our lives for us to judge or indoctrinate or change. God is sending them to us to *love*. When true love is prevalent and when weary, lost people genuinely

sense it, God will do the judging; the doctrine will come, and He will work any necessary changes—all in His time.

This is an abiding principle as well as an active principle. When we *abide,* we dwell within; consequently, when we *abide* in Him, His love dwells within us. *"...love builds up... The man who loves God and is known by God" (I Corinthians 8:1-2).* When we exercise this love that is abiding within us, we will *actively* pursue building up one another. *"Dear friends, since God so loved us, we also ought to love one another" (I John 4:11).*

In the Old Testament we read that these admonitions have foundations in the Levitical law: *"The stranger who resides with you shall be to you as the native among you, and you shall love him as yourself..." (Leviticus 19:34).* What an admonition! This love is abiding, and it is active. We can't help ourselves! When His love is abiding within us we are *compelled*, and we are *constrained* to reach out with arms of love and embrace the lives of the weary travelers who come our way regardless of how they look, think, or act!

Their physical and spiritual and emotional conditions are incidental! Jesus didn't take these things into consideration when He said, *"Your sins are forgiven; go and sin no more...,"* so why should these things be of significance to us? He socialized with tax collectors and prostitutes and beggars and lepers and sinners! Are we fearful of what people will think if we are seen with a "sinner?" Do we have some sort of *spiritual* image that we feel is essential to uphold? Are we fearful that somehow their *sinfulness* will tarnish our superior, holy exterior?

Six years ago my husband took a position as a religion professor at a Christian university in Nashville. We moved there just before school started, and for the first time since we had been young seminarians, we moved into an apartment while we were building a house.

Other than a foster brother who lived near Nashville with his wife, I didn't know a single person there. It was lonely! The very first week my husband was on the job we were to attend a banquet for the college faculty. Having all the vanities of any normal American woman, I determined that it was vital to look my best for all these people that I didn't know. So I went on a mission—a mission for a beauty shop.

I drove down the street away from our little apartment and stopped at the first beauty shop I saw. As beauty shops go, it wasn't much. It was in a little strip mall and was one of the chain varieties that take walk-ins. What I walked into that day was much more than an ordinary beauty shop. I had no appointment, but this visit was indeed a *"divine appointment."*

My beautician that day was lonelier than I. That didn't seem possible, but it was! She was about my age, recently divorced, embittered by the whole process, uprooted, away from her family, working hard just to pay the rent, and all alone. Wonder of wonders, though, she and I became fast friends—and are to this day!

Often during the four years we lived in Nashville, my beautician and I would meet together after work and share a meal at a local restaurant. We would discuss children, futures, and the things that make ordinary life special. What's so unusual about that, you might ask? My dear friend *smokes* Yes, the "S"

word. What section of the restaurant do you suppose we sat in? You guessed it—*The SMOKING SECTION!*

Did I like it? Not particularly! Actually, not at ALL! One day while we were eating, it dawned on me that it was possible that I might be *seen* there in the SMOKING SECTION by some of the Christian college professors or students. What would *they* think? Just as quickly as that thought came to me, another followed. Yes, it was important what the Christian community thought of me. And *that* was the reason I was sitting in the SMOKING SECTION.

I was a Christian and was carrying His love to my friend. My *true* Christian friends could think nothing but good thoughts about my mission, and those who might think otherwise were not for me to contend with. Do you comprehend this? My implication is not that

> *God is the judge of those things, and He is also the judge of the human heart!*

my friend was wrong; she knew the Lord in a personal way. She was a SMOKER! God is the judge of those things, and He is also the judge of the human heart!

A few years ago one of the major world relief organizations had a slogan that has persistently continued to ring in my ears since the day I first heard it. It was simple, but profound; it was elementary, but complex; it was convicting, and it was compelling: *"IF ONLY ALL THE HANDS THAT REACH COULD TOUCH!"* It's that simple and elementary, but it is so very convicting and compelling that I just can't get away from it.

We have one major responsibility to those who come through and into our lives. We *must* be like the family in the Portland airport and extend nonjudgmental arms of love and acceptance. Then, we must take a step forward and be like my counterpart that day in the airport. As we embrace the people who enter our lives, our sincere expression of love should be pure and simple: *"Welcome to the family of God. Jesus Christ is all the good things people say He is and a whole lot more!*

Chapter 6
A Vessel of Honor

Those of us who name the name of Christ as our personal Savior are very cognizant of the Great Commission: *"Go ye, therefore, into all the world and preach the good news to all creation" (Mark 16:15).* We have no quarrel with Jesus' words here and honor His commission. The rub comes, though, when we (being even more aware and cognizant of our own lives, human errors, sins, and weaknesses) try to comprehend the application of His commission. Somehow we just can't flesh this out into our own lives and, therefore, project its commands and demands on the *professionals*—pastors, missionaries, and *called ones.*

Paul understood our human plight and dilemma, for by his own admission he was the "chiefest of sinners." Before his miraculous and dramatic conversion, he had been an adamant and active persecutor of Christians, utilizing his position and exercising his great intellect to wage a literal war against them. And then one day, the unimaginable

happened! Paul himself was brought to his knees with a staggering blow of humbling proportions when he was confounded by a blinding light on the road to Damascas. Finally, after Paul's eyesight was restored, he got a handle on this miraculous treasure and the urgency placed on him to share the Great Commission commanded by Christ.

In II Corinthians chapter four Paul talks about the light that shines out of darkness directly into our hearts. Then in II Corinthians 4:7 he lowers the boom on all of us: *"We have this treasure in jars of clay to prove that this all surpassing power is from God and not from us!"* As Christians we simply don't have a choice; we are responsible to carry the treasure.

At our house there is only one kind of flower as far as my husband is concerned, and that is the rhododendron. He is from the State of Washington, and the "rhoddy" is the Washington State flower. In over three decades of marriage, he has learned the names of three other flowers—the rose, the carnation, and (my favorite) the iris. But, otherwise, the word *flower* for him is synonymous with rhododendron.

Rhododendrons are absolutely beautiful, hardy flowers that bloom in the spring and come in assorted shades of white, pink, and red. When their bushes are blooming, they can be breathtakingly beautiful in the Northwest springtime. If you were to come to our home in the spring, and I had a bouquet of rhododendrons displayed on my dining room table, your first response would most likely be, *"My, what beautiful flowers!"*

This all seems so simple in the realm of flowers. It seems so natural and right. But when it comes to spiritual things, we Christians often really goof up here. Never has a guest come to my home, seen a bouquet of "rhoddies" and exclaimed, "My what a beautiful vase!" It is the flowers that are observed and praised. Rhododendrons are so innately beautiful that the container that holds them is irrelevant compared to their beauty. They could be in a gorgeous crystal vase, a clay pot, or a mayonnaise jar, and they would still be just as breathtakingly beautiful.

> *Never has a guest come to my home, seen a bouquet of "rhoddies" and exclaimed, "My what a beautiful vase!"*

Spiritually, the implication here is so very clear—until we get about the business of fleshing out the message that *"Christ in us is indeed the hope of glory,"* we aren't living the Great Commission. It is not the vessel that gets the praise, it is the treasure. This is not a comparison between the vase and the treasure, but rather it is a contrast. The very simplicity and humanness of the vessel only serves to better accentuate the beauty of the treasure.

For many years I have been a teacher, and a good deal of the time I have taught English. In English there are eight different parts of speech, and each one has a specific use. An adjective describes a noun, and a verb can be turned into an adjective by changing it into a "verbal." Thus, we could have an *honored* vessel. The preposition is a small word that shows comparison between two nouns. In school

the teacher would often illustrate this by holding a book *above* the desk, *below* the desk, *beside* the desk, *in* the desk, *between* the desks, *under* the desk, etc. Thus, we could have a vessel *of* honor.

On the surface this little differentiation may seem insignificant, but in reality these two are worlds apart. When we grasp the true concept of *II Corinthians 4:7* (jars *of* clay), rather than thinking that we should be *honored*, then we are set free to acknowledge the unfathomable truth that this message will never transfer to a hurt and dying world until each one of us professing Christians recognizes that with all our flaws and human weaknesses, we still have been *chosen* to carry this remarkable treasure. The implication of this scripture is that we are *"good enough"* to carry Jesus Christ *in* us.

The problem here lies in our conscious awareness of our humanity. Not many of us are a "benediction as we arrive." We actually trip, get our skirt caught in our panty hose, say the wrong thing, or have a bad hair day. We are all so very ordinary. Great!

When we truly come to acknowledge and accept our ordinary humanity, then this unbelievable comparison can begin to come into play. Our society and churches have many Christians who have such a low self-concept and esteem

> *When we truly come to acknowledge and accept our ordinary humanity, then this unbelievable comparison can begin to come into play.*

that they never even entertain a passing thought that they could indeed be the *only* vessel to carry His amazing treasure to a perishing Samaritan along their path.

This is simply nothing but a mystery. How can you and I, mere humans as we are with all our flaws, blemishes, and frailties ever be worthy to carry the treasure. And what is the treasure anyway? *Colossians 1:26-27* answers that question this way: *"...the mystery that has been kept hidden for ages and generations, but is now disclosed to the saints. To them God has chosen to make known among the Gentiles the glorious riches of this mystery, which is Christ in you, the hope of glory."* Do you hear it? Can you see it? This miracle is for us—the Gentiles. Before Christ, it had been a secret, but now the word is out. And what is that word? *Christ is in us so we can become the hope of glory.*

As Christians (like Paul), we just must get a handle on this. There aren't enough of the paid folks to carry this remarkable treasure to a dying world. A few years ago a Florida jetliner went down in the Potomac River right in the middle of Washington D.C. For some strange reason I had my television on that afternoon and was getting ready to pick up my children from school. Suddenly, this news release broke through all the scheduled programming.

Without even realizing it, I found myself seated in the middle of my living room floor, totally engaged in the drama that was unfolding live before my eyes. As I sat there that day, suspended between Washington D.C. and El Paso, Texas, with no concept of anything but this live drama, I saw a helicopter hover overhead as a young stewardess

was going down into the icy winter waters for the third time.

At the same time, I saw an unnamed bystander on the shore rip off his jacket, swim out to her, and help her grab the line that was being dangled so precariously from the helicopter. As I sat there that day, I heard another voice in addition to the newsmen on the television; that voice was saying, "Hang on lady, hang on!" When I took a double take to see where the voice was coming from, I realized that the voice I heard was my own!

What a thrill! She was rescued! When they brought her up to safety out of that water and certain death, she had only words of praise and "thank yous" for the helicopter pilot and the citizen who had worked together to rescue her from the river. Not once did she question whether her rescuers had been to the Red Cross life saving classes; not once did she mention their education; not once did she question their gender; not once did she question their ethnicity. No! She was going down for the last time; she saw a hand, grabbed it and held on for dear life!

That early winter afternoon, sitting on the floor of my living room, the Holy Spirit taught me again a vital spiritual lesson about my mission. If there had been even seconds of hesitation on the part of the bystander on the shore or by the helicopter, that young stewardess would have been another casualty that day. She saw a hand, asked no questions, only grabbed it and held on for her life.

If we as Christians are so unsure of our capabilities that we hesitate for even one minute, someone may go down

for the last time with no hope. We don't have time to call the preacher or get more schooling ourselves. But if we are present, we are compelled and empowered to extend a hand—whether unprepared or feeble or unsure or frail—and allow that person the marvelous privilege of sharing in this remarkable *"hope of glory"* which is Christ in us.

The people in your life who you meet during the week will care very little about how often you go to church, or how beautifully you can sing in the choir, or how eloquent your "testimony" is before other Christians, or what seminary you might have attended, or how important your parents may be in a specific denomination. These things are important and have their place, but they must never be *first place*.

The people in your life, however, will know if you are a vessel *of* honor willing to carry this incredible treasure to their dying and hurting lives. Talk about the Great Commission! Our problem as Christian isn't that we don't know what we are supposed to do. We just don't have confidence that the Holy Spirit will empower us in ways that far supercede our humanity.

Six years ago I had the opportunity and privilege of visiting Israel for the first time. This journey so impacted my life spiritually, that I have been back three times since. Nothing, though, will ever equal the thrill of that first journey to the Holy Land.

One day as we were driving south from Qumran and Masada toward the Dead Sea, our guide pointed out the right window of the bus to an extremely long, flat, high

bluff. "You see that mesa up there," she said. "In the time of Christ, there was a village up on that bluff. This is the place Jesus was referring to in Matthew 5."

Immediately my mind returned to the Sermon on the Mount when Jesus said, *"...You are the light of the world. A city on a hill cannot be hidden. Neither do people light a lamp and put it under a bowl. Instead they put it on its stand, and it gives light to everyone in the house. In the same way, let your light shine before men, that they may see your good deeds and praise your Father in heaven"* *Matthew 5:14-16.*

Suddenly, that hot day in a tourist bus I got it! *I am a city on a hill.* Can you get it? Does it make sense? When we are a vessel **of** honor, we cannot help but be a light on the hill. Despite our "humanness," people will know that that there is something winsome and unique and different about us. This is not about us, but it is about

> **Suddenly, there that hot day in a tourist bus I got it! I am a city on a hill. Can you get it?**

this marvelous treasure that we are chosen and privileged to carry. Once again, it is a contrast—not a comparison!

Too many "Christians" read this scripture incorrectly. They read, *"...In the same way, let your light shine before men, that they may see your good deeds and the pastor may praise you Sunday morning before the entire church body, or if you really shine, he might put your name in the bulletin, etc."* This attitude—which is prevalent among

some Christians—stifles the message and draws attention to the vessel, not the treasure. We don't need a "byline;" not everyone has to

> *We don't need a "by-line;" not everyone has to know every wonderful deed we have done...*

know every wonderful deed we have done in the name of Christ.

Our true and final reward comes when we are glorified with him and we hear those coveted words, *"Well done thou good and faithful servant," (KJV).* Hearing these words from the Master Himself are all the reward a true Christian ever yearns for. Years ago, when the bystander was interviewed after "rescuing" the stewardess, he didn't think he had done anything out of the ordinary or had performed in a way that couldn't have been done hundreds of others. He just happened to be in that place at that time; he had the treasure (which was life), and he extended it to a drowning human being.

In one of our family's moves, I was forced to take a job that wasn't really the one I wanted. But since we had a mortgage to pay and it *was* a job, I took it! It was a difficult, stressful job, but I decided to make the best of it until something better was available. How was I to know that this job was indeed my Great Commission—at least for that time—and that through my life would march a family that knew *nothing* of this remarkable treasure, but desperately needed a willing vessel to carry that treasure to them?

On the very first day of orientation for that new job—which I didn't even want and where I didn't even want to be—I met a new friend. She was assigned to work in the same building as I.

> **Before the coffee break was over on that first day of orientation, she had shared with me a sad and heartbreaking story...**

Before the coffee break was over on that first day of orientation, she had shared with me a sad and heartbreaking story of her life. Things had never been easy for her since her childhood, and they certainly weren't easy for her then. She had just gone through a painful divorce, had moved to a new state to rebuild her life, bringing her two young daughters and her teenager with her.

By the third day of that first week, she casually dropped into our conversations that in addition to her divorce and this relocation, she was in remission from serious cancer. She talked about her cancer and previous surgeries with a rather casual tone in her voice, but the look in her eyes was all too revealing. Here I was at a job I didn't want to take, in a place I would rather not be, but with an opportunity to be a vessel despite those circumstances.

One Friday afternoon of the second or third week of that new job, my new friend walked right into my face and said, "I need a hug." Very seldom is something that clear. After we hugged, she and I walked arm in arm downstairs, got a coke, and chatted a bit. In passing, I remarked that I thought she might like my church.

Much to my surprise, she was there the next Sunday and came several times afterwards. My husband and I took her and the little girls our for dinner, and both of us fell in love with them almost immediately. There was something urgent and ominous about them that was beyond us, but we could both feel it. Like a magnate we were drawn to them.

A couple weeks after she visited our church for the first time, she came to me and said that the doctors had found another malignancy. They needed to remove it surgically, but it didn't seem to be a big deal. She would just be *in-and-out* of the hospital. Then she asked me if I would be willing to take her to the hospital and be her *family.* Do you get it? I was honored! Here I was in a place I didn't want to be, doing a job that I really didn't want to do, but still God was able to use my feeble, human, marred vessel.

It was in October that she and I made that first trip to the hospital. She was right; she was just *in-and-out,* and although she treated the experience as though it were nothing, I had a premonition that there was more to her condition than either she or I wanted to face.

Her background was nearly heathen. Her birth father had been a Nazi storm trooper, and her mother had had several different husbands and lovers! Her mother had brought her to the United States when she was a young girl, and her childhood was peppered with trips back and forth between her mother and various foster homes. Despite all life's obstacles, there was something in her that hungered for an education which somehow, she had attained. In fact, she had a master's degree and had served as a school principal in another state.

Her marriage was certainly not one "made in heaven," and after three daughters and years of verbal abuse, she finally divorced and moved to be near one of her several half-brothers. The divorce had been less than amicable, leaving her bitter, disillusioned, nearly broke—but determined to jumpstart her life and provide for her children.

By Christmas of that year, she was returning to the hospital on a weekly basis for radiation, and it was all too evident that the cancer was spreading rapidly. I watched my friend make a valiant effort to come to work when most people wouldn't have even considered it.

Her cancer returned with a vengeance and by the first days of February, she could hardly maneuver the halls of the school. The treatments made her nauseous, and she began to lose her hair. Often I would see her between classes on her knees in the restroom heaving, watch her get up, smile, and attempt to make it through one more class. She tried to negotiate with a walker and even with a wheel chair, but finally, she had to face the inevitable and take a medical leave from work.

> *Her cancer returned with a vengeance...*

Early in our relationship, I asked her permission to allow our Sunday School class to bring in food, help with the children, and take her to her many doctors and clinic appointments. At first she was reluctant, but as she began to feel the genuine love from many of us, she became acceptant and finally dependent on our class.

Our class approached this opportunity for service with a willingness that I have never seen duplicated. EVERYONE helped. One lady organized regular, balanced meals; several of us took turns taking the little girls over the weekends; and one lady in particular became her constant, vigilant companion. It was the early church in action in the twentieth century—truly a beautiful sight to behold.

Her situation, though, was not beautiful. Thanks to the concentrated help of many of us, she was able to hang on tenaciously to her custody of the little girls until the end of that school year when their dad was to get them for the summer. That was indeed a summer to remember for all of us involved in her life. Although her physical condition weakened rapidly,

> *Although her physical condition weakened rapidly, her spirit seemed to soar.*

her spirit seemed to soar. She was a woman with a mission. And that mission was simply this: to be able to see the little girls one more time in the fall.

Toward midsummer she was taking daily radiation treatments and had been in the hospital more times than any of us could count. Her house was converted into a hospital of its own, equipped with hospital bed, oxygen, wheel chair ramps. There were daily visits from one lady in particular and many of us in general as we tried everything we knew to be *Jesus* to her. As long as she was able, she would allow her one friend to bring her to church in her wheelchair. It was an effort, but one well worth it!

I was out of town a great deal that summer, but regularly visited her in the hospital and her home when I was in town. Toward the first of August, many of us who were close to her were apprehensive about whether she would reach her goal of seeing her two little girls one last time. She was daily getting weaker and weaker, and day by day she was losing her agonizing battle against cancer. At one of these times when she seemed the lowest my husband and I were preparing to leave town for a week. I really wasn't certain whether she would be alive or not when I returned, and it was important to me to know where she was spiritually.

So it was that on one particular afternoon I went to the hospital determined that I would not leave town until I had made an opportunity to talk with her about spiritual things. Now, *I* was a woman with a mission! Finally, after we had been interrupted by the doctor, nurses, social worker, and even pastors from the church, she and I were alone.

I called her by name, and hesitantly said, "None of us has any certainty about the future. I could walk out of here today and it could be over for me in a second. I've come to love you not because you're sick, but because you're my friend. Despite all my human frailties, I plan to make it to heaven, and I'd like to know that you'll be there too." Then I looked directly into her eyes and asked, "As best as you understand it, have you made peace with God?"

Without a moment's hesitation she came right back at me, "Of course I have." Her eyes were intent, and she was blunt and to the point with her most disarming nature. "I signed one of those cards at your church!" During all those months of

visitations and expressions of love and human concern, something eternal had transpired in her heart. There had been a divine connection; her life had been forever changed.

We had been endeavoring to ease her physical suffering and to minister to her earthly needs and in so doing she had seen Jesus and had come to know Him in a way that was personal and fit her background and degree of understanding. Although my heart was heavy about her physical situation, I was walking on air that day as I left the hospital, rejoicing in her confession of a spiritual relationship. What a blessing!

The girls did come with their grandmother sometime in early August. My friend was so weak by this time that she could hardly raise her hairless head from her pillow. But, she reached within herself to a reservoir of strength beyond anyone's comprehension, put on her wig and makeup, and prepared for their visit as though she were a high school girl attending the prom.

> *She reached within herself to a reservoir of strength beyond anyone's comprehension...*

There was almost a giddiness about her anticipation. When these two little blue-eyed blondes arrived in her hospital room; it was a sacred moment. My husband lifted one up on each side of her bed, and with one child on either side of her, she pulled them to her, and we all heard her say, "I've kept alive all summer just for these hugs!" There wasn't a dry eye in that room that day!

Within just a couple days of the girls' departure, she began to slip in and out of a coma. For two weeks she struggled and rallied, and then each time slipped a little lower. During her final two weeks there was not a single moment that she was alone, for throughout the entire time—twenty-four hours a day—someone from our church was there with her.

Finally, on my first day back to work one year and six days after I had met my friend for the first time, I went with hesitation to the hospital to see her. She had been in a deep coma all day and hadn't responded to anyone. I leaned down to her ear and spoke her name. As I did, she opened her eyes and reached up her arms to me.

Gently, I took her in my arms and held her exhausted, disease-racked frame. Quietly, I quoted the *23rd Psalm*, and then my mind returned to *John 14: "Let not your heart be troubled, neither let it be afraid. In my father's house are many mansions. If it were not so I would have told you. I go to prepare a place for you... that where I am there you may be also" (KJV)*. I laid her back on the pillows, kissed her forehead, and left, knowing in my heart that that would most likely be our last visit before heaven! And two hours later she was gone—from this earth, but not from my heart or remembrance.

As I was driving Rose to the hospital for a treatment the week before she died, she had shared with me some of her plans for her memorial service. She knew what music she wanted; she wanted my husband to conduct the service; and she requested that three of us who had been close each

give a tribute. As I sat at my computer trying to compose my thoughts about this incredible journey God had allowed me to take that had lasted only one year and one week from the day I met this total stranger, I was confounded.

Sitting at my computer that day there began to form a transformation in my thoughts. My dear friend, Rose, had given much more back to me and the others in her life than any of us had been able to give to her. We had started out to give, but instead, we had received. Here are some of the words of tribute God gave me that

> *Rose had given much more back to me and the others in her life than any of us had been able to give to her.*

day to share with her family and to honor her life:

As I have gone through my life, often I have asked myself how I could minister for Jesus. *In Matthew 25: 35-40,* Jesus Himself teaches us how: *"For I was hungry and you gave me something to eat, I was thirsty and you gave me something to drink, I was a stranger and you invited me in. I needed clothes and you clothed me, I was sick and you looked after me... Then the righteous will answer him, 'Lord when did we see you hungry and feed you, or thirsty and give you something to drink? When did we see you a stranger and invite you in, or needing clothes and clothe you? When did we see you sick ...and go to visit you?' The King will reply, 'I tell you the truth, whatever you did for one of the least of these brothers of mine, you did for me."*

Through her illness, Rose came to a conscious acceptance of Christ as her personal Savior; this made her His sister. So, although many times during my life, I feel I have failed in serving Him, I believe that this time God used me and many others to actually minister *to* Christ by helping Rose.

Around my parents' patio, my mother has cultivated over a dozen of the most gorgeous rose bushes I have ever seen. Recently, when I was visiting my parents in Idaho, I went out one night to trim the roses around their patio. There was every imaginable color in full bloom, but there were many blooms that had wilted and needed to be trimmed so that other flowers could take their place. My father explained to me that I should cut the roses back quite far so that new blooms would continue to blossom for the rest of the summer.

In a sense, God has trimmed back the blossoms of Rose's life, but the part that is left is the part that I want to remember for the rest of my life. Gone is the pain, and the oxygen, and the radiation, and the chemo, and the IVs, and the constant bed confinement, and the wig, and the wheel chair, and the walker, and the discomfort of being able to do nothing for herself, and the pills, and most of all the pain.

What blossoms in my heart is her spirit, her will to live, her undying devotion and love for three daughters, her abrupt sense of humor, her friendship. Rose's death is a loss to her girls and to all of us, but she is our deposit in Heaven. She is with friends and family who have gone before, walking on her own and free of all pain and humiliation of her sickness.

I have been blessed beyond what words could ever explain to have known Rose. **She became Jesus to me this past year**, and I shall ever be grateful for the privilege of helping her just a little and for all the lessons she taught me. Thanks, my friend!

If I had waited for one of the "paid guys" to lead Rose to the Lord, she might never have made it, because they were simply not in her life. *I was!* It was just that simple. I didn't choose the situation; God did! God sent me into her life or her into my life. Whichever way—it was a divine encounter!

This isn't about me. It's about Him. We are worthy. We are chosen. We are good enough to carry this remarkable treasure which is *"...Jesus Christ in us the hope of glory."* We are able to carry this treasure in our human jars of clay to prove that this all-surpassing power is not from us, but rather from him. It's not a comparison; it's a contrast! Christ Jesus gets all the glory and all the praise!

Enjoy the glory, Rose!

Chapter 7
The Smithsonian Chair

When our daughter, Dana, was a junior in college she began ~~to began~~ to develop symptoms of a chemical disorder that affected her entire endocrinological system. At first none of us considered her situation serious or critical; rather, we attributed her symptoms to typical college stress of a very active, high-achieving student. When her symptoms continued for three or four months, though, we all decided that she should at least have a routine physical checkup. The checkup showed her to be a healthy twenty-year old with no significant problems of any sort. What a relief!

Dana had a double major of drama and literature and for her entire college career remained an honor student, graduating with the highest honors. Since she was a drama student she was involved in *all* the school dramatic productions of any sort. She attended college in Southern California, and we were living at the time in West Texas,

so her dad and I took turns going to California to see her latest production.

It was after one of these productions that she went for a checkup with her father. When he got the good news of her healthy condition, he happily took the next flight home on Monday morning. He and I were blithely going about the routines of a normal Tuesday when I received a phone call from Dana in my office as assistant principal of the local high school.

I could tell by the sound of her voice that she was alarmed, and that alarmed me! At her checkup on Monday the doctor had taken some routine blood samples, and apparently there was something highly abnormal that appeared in her blood. Dana was in the office of an endocrinologist when she called, and at the time none of the three of us could hardly even pronounce the word. My hand began to tremble and my body chilled as I tried to come to terms with the words I was hearing over the long-distance telephone wire.

> *My hand began to tremble and my body chilled as I tried to come to terms with the words I was hearing over the long-distance telephone wire.*

It didn't make any sense. Just two days ago the doctor had said she was a perfectly healthy, normal twenty year old, and today...! Finally, the doctor himself got on the line and explained to me that it was the *prolactin* count in her blood that had triggered the alarm. In a young woman

of her age, this count is normally "30," but Dana's was "330!" The doctors were *positive* she had a serious problem, and they were reasonably certain from their knowledge of this prolactin count that she had a pituitary tumor! They assured us all it was small and could be gone in months.

That evening was one of the most somber and frightening evenings my husband and I have ever spent together. We vaguely knew about the pituitary gland and had a basic layman's understanding of its purpose. Neither of us was positive where it is located in the brain, and we had certainly never given a minute's thought to *prolactin count.*

Suddenly, the pituitary and prolactin count (which we had never once discussed in all our years of marriage) took on overwhelming significance to us that night— significance of gigantic proportion! This was our "baby," hundreds of miles away from us, facing a crisis, and we weren't there. Five years previously my husband had lost his stepfather to a brain tumor that took his life within six weeks of its diagnosis. Thus, we had a particularly heightened concern level that night.

What had begun as a typical day became a hallmark day in the life of our family! Dana was the calmest of the three of us. She just took this in stride with typical youthful confidence of a positive tomorrow! Dana was amazing!

The doctor informed us all that they would immediately perform an MRI, but he was relatively confident that the tumor was small enough that it could be shrunk and dissipated with drug therapy. A few days later when the

MRI was taken, it revealed a tumor about the size of a bing cherry—much larger than even the optimistic doctor had anticipated. At that time, he gave Dana two choices: the first choice was strong drug therapy, and the second was surgery. The doctor strongly advocated the drug therapy, and Dana opted for that since she felt that it would not interrupt her college education.

And so she began that day a very long journey—one much longer than any of us had suspected or anticipated. Initially, the drugs were supposed to shrink the tumor within six months, but that never happened. For the rest of her college years, and the first two years of graduate school, Dana stayed on a rigorous and extreme drug regimen. Every six months or so she had to submit to yet another MRI to study the current condition of the tumor. The dosages of the drug she was taking were so large that nearly daily they caused her to have "morning sickness" symptoms.

> *Initially, the drugs were supposed to shrink the tumor within six months, but that never happened.*

During the entire four-year ordeal, no one ever heard her complain even once, nor did her "condition" keep her from maintaining her active college and graduate school life or keeping her grades at the very highest level. Once again, she was amazing! Dana just seemed to take this all in stride as though it were a common occurrence of many people!

When Dana graduated from college she pursued her life long dream of acting. All her good grades and hard work landed her a much-coveted slot in San Francisco at the American Conservatory Theatre graduate school. She loved her life and work there in San Francisco, but her "condition" was always hovering above her, demanding to be dealt with and not ignored.

For two summers during graduate school, Dana acted in the Boise Shakespeare Festival in Idaho and loved that just as much as her work in San Francisco. During her second summer in Idaho, Dana made a decision that the drug therapy was never going to solve her problem. Since there was no one ever recorded who had taken such high dosages of her medication over such an extended period of time there were haunting questions about its long term residual affects. Consequently, Dana decided that she would return to San Francisco and have the surgery in September as soon as her summer acting contract was completed.

Dana had been seeing an outstanding doctor in San Francisco who had pioneered a "miracle" operation for pituitary tumors. Rather than shave the head, cut the scalp, and lift out the brain, his surgery is called "transsphenoidal." The technique goes under the upper lip, through the sphenoid passages, and retrieves the tumor almost in a remote control process. With this procedure, a patient exits major brain surgery with no outward sign but a drip pad under his/her nose. It is truly a "miracle" operation!

After nearly four years of drug therapy and anticipation that the tumor would shrink, Dana's surgery was scheduled

for September 29, 1996, at the University of California Hospital in San Francisco. Her father and I were now living in Tennessee, so the two of us took off from work and flew to San Francisco to be with her and to bring her home for recuperation when she was able to travel.

The day of the surgery we were told to be at the hospital by 6:00 AM and to be prepared for surgery when called. The doctor who did this "miracle" surgery scheduled these operations for Fridays, and the waiting room was *filled* with people of all ages waiting for this same operation. Suddenly, Dana's *rare* condition appeared common as we sat among strangers (some as far away from home as South America) each waiting his or her turn for the same "miracle" that we hoped Dana would receive. The waiting became interminable as one by one others were called for their surgery, but it wasn't until after 3:00 PM that Dana was taken for her operation.

Since Dana was one of the last patients that day, she wasn't returned from post op until early evening. Together my husband and I talked with the doctor, and he assured us that he was relatively confident that all her tumor had been extracted. Finally, around 9:00 PM, Dana was returned to her private room, and between us, David and I decided that I would take the first shift and stay through the night with Dana while he went back to our lodging for some much needed sleep.

It had been an extremely, long exhausting day! Truthfully, the last four years had played a heavy toll on us all for the threat of this tumor and its potential serious

ramifications had always been present in our minds and hearts. At last, we were nearing the end of a long, dark family tunnel—a journey that had been begun with trepidation and anxiety, but was now

> *...we were nearing the end of a long, dark family tunnel...*

ending in hope. All that was left was simply to get through the next couple days of hospitalization, make the plane trip home, and complete the recuperation period!

For four years we had been focused—100 percent focused—on our daughter's condition. To the best of our ability we had accessed the very best medical help available for her; there had been many prayers on her behalf; and overall, our family had done our best to be supportive and understanding of her unspoken fears and concerns.

Around 10:00 PM that evening the nurse had Dana settled as comfortably as possible after major surgery. I asked the nurse if she could provide me with a cot or small bed so that I could be with Dana all night to attend any of her needs. Shortly, the nurse returned to the room and apologetically explained that she could find no available cots or beds, but proffered me a contraption that bore a distant resemblance to a chair.

The "chair" the nurse provided looked as though it had come directly from a 1950s genre nursing home. It had a high back and wooden arms that protruded at right angles on each side. The front folded down hinting at a reclining feature, and along the right side there was a lever that

appeared to be intended to engage the same reclining feature. Its yellowish, Naugahyde leather was cracked, pealing, stained, and dirty! Overall, this device provided a pitiful, dilapidated facsimile of a "chair." If I hadn't been so tired and exhausted, it would have been comical. As a whole, "the chair" was a perfect candidate for a Smithsonian exhibit. Then and there, I mentally dubbed this contraption the *Smithsonian chair!*

The nurse provided me with a pillow, some sheets, and a blanket, explaining that I could recline and rest in this chair throughout the rest of the night. As the nurse left the room, my challenge began. Once I was sure that Dana was comfortable, I approached "the chair." I put the sheet over its length, placed the pillow behind my head, held the blanket over me with my left hand, and reached with my right hand to engage the reclining device.

The first challenge that presented itself to me was the discomfort caused by the chair's wooden arms. When the chair was in its complete reclining position, the arms served as perfect projectiles into my sides. Thus, I repositioned "the chair" in its upright position and went on a search for two pillows to place on either side of me. When I had secured these two additional pillows, I repeated the same three steps I had used the first time I had reclined "the chair."

This time, though, I held both elbows close to my sides in order to keep these two additional pillows from falling to the floor when the chair was reclined. This presented quite a challenge especially for my right arm and hand because not only did I need my right elbow to hold the

pillow in place, but I needed my right hand for activating the reclining lever. But I wasn't settled yet!

Somewhere in the progression of reclining "the chair" from its total upright position to its completed reclining position, there was a notch that if hit exactly, caused "the chair" to double as an ejection seat, shooting me straight to my feet as though I were a rocketlike projectile.

> **There was a notch that if hit exactly caused "the chair" to double as an ejection seat...**

Several such launchings sent me on a search of yet another pillow. After a number of aborted attempts and trials and errors regarding the exact placement of this additional pillow, I discovered that when this pillow was placed behind me precisely in the small of my back, I could successfully maneuver "the chair" past its launching notch to its complete reclining position.

Now I added yet another step in my process of adjusting "the chair" in order to rest. This process had become so complicated that just learning and remembering the correct sequencing of the procedure required a great deal of mental adeptness and finesse within itself. You get the picture! I was literally *bonded* with that stupid chair and could have easily tied Lucille Ball for comic relief.

There was one major hitch in this whole process. Dana. I had become so consumed with "the chair" and the proper manipulating of its controls, and had become so proud of my success with it that I had begun to resent Dana's needs and comfort. This process was all very subtle, but I began

to notice that when Dana would ask for me or give some indication of discomfort that I would hesitate to attend her.

At first my hesitations were slight and imperceptible, but as the hours wore on, I became more and more resentful of her *interruptions* and less willing to disengage "the chair" and take care of the business that had brought me into this hospital room one thousand miles from my home! Sometime between 2:00 and 3:00 AM, the Lord began to speak to me about all this.

When put into proper perspective, the entire situation seemed humorous. "The chair" was unimportant, inconsequential. Dana was my primary focus; *she* was the reason I was in San Francisco and in this particular hospital room! *She* was what was important; *she* was the one I had committed myself to over twenty-four years earlier; she was the one with the needs; *she* was the one so many people had prayed for.

> *"The chair" was inconsequential. Dana was my primary focus; she was the reason I was in San Francisco...*

The rest of the night sailed smoothly as I "rested in the Lord" and attended my daughter's needs without regard for my own comfort and the proper manipulation of "the chair." In retrospect, that entire night is humorous, and it's fun to remember "the chair," but there is an important, vital lesson that I was reminded of that night in San Francisco. We begin each day, week, year, marriage, relationship, etc. with high hopes and great plans.

But life in its inevitability has a way of distracting us, and often distracting us very quickly from noble goals and worthwhile objectives. It is so easy to put our attention on some interruption that appears along the pathway to our goals, and often we get so confused that we think this new distraction *is* our goal. When this happens, we can become discouraged, confused, frustrated, and even angry.

The Gospel of Luke records a true story about this phenomenon in *Chapter 10:38-42: "As Jesus and his disciples were on their way, he came to a village where a woman named Martha opened her home to him. She had a sister called Mary, who sat at the Lord's feet listening to what he said. But Martha was distracted by all the preparations that had to be made. She came to him and asked, 'Lord, don't you care that my sister has left me to do the work by myself? Tell her to help me!' 'Martha, Martha,' the Lord answered, 'you are worried and upset about many things, but only one thing is needed. Mary has chosen what is better, and it will not be taken away from her.'"*

Here was Jesus Himself making a "pastoral call" in the home of Lazarus, Mary, and Martha. What an honor! He chose their place to rest His weary body after walking miles and teaching many. They were both delighted with Jesus' visit, and both Mary and Martha responded within the framework of her own personality. Martha had to get the house clean and prepare a meal because an important guest was in their home. But Mary dropped all she was doing to spend time with Jesus.

Nothing was wrong with what Martha was doing, but she messed up in a royal manner! Martha expected Mary

to respond in the same way she did, and when Mary dropped everything to sit down and fellowship with Jesus leaving Martha with all the myriads of preparations, Martha became frustrated, bitter, angry, and full of self-pity.

There was a lot of things right about what Martha did that day. She had the right motives: She wanted to please Christ and provide a comfortable, warm place for Him to rest His weary body. She had the right actions: everything was right

> *If Martha had the right motives and actions, what got her so upset?*

with Martha's preparations in cleaning the house and preparing the best meal possible for this honored guest. Martha's actions weren't wrong; they were right! If Martha had the right motives and actions, what got her so upset?

Martha had the wrong focus! Verse 40 says she was *distracted* by the preparations that she felt had to be made and made at once! She was so distracted that she had the audacity to come to the Lord and demand that He tell Mary to help her! Have you ever heard yourself talking to the Lord like Martha? Martha's words remind me of a portion of an old song: *"I've worked so hard for Jesus; I often boast and say: I've sacrificed a lot of things to walk the narrow way. I gave up fame and fortune; I'm worth a lot to thee."*

Like the song writer and like Martha, we have our focus off center. Our personal comfort isn't the reason we are called to follow Him; we are called to follow Him and serve others! Preparation is vital and important, but there comes a time

when we must be totally centered on Him. Mary had it! Few of us ever achieve her simplicity. That's the lesson the Lord attempted to teach me that early morning in San Francisco. Something as silly and insignificant as a stupid chair can divert our attention from the real reason for our existence.

There are consequences for all of our actions whether we are responding like Mary or reacting like Martha. As we go through our lives, we can become so distracted by our focus on our right motives and actions that we fail to see the vital importance of little things that we label distractions. Many parents of adult children, for example, have looked back on things that they thought were distractions when their children were smaller—school events, ball games, PTA, recitals, homework, just listening, etc.—and wished that they just had one day to be distracted again. But those times come, and then they go forever.

Or, we start out enthusiastically on a project of service or in an effort to witness to a non-Christian neighbor or family member. All too many times we lose heart and in so doing, lose focus. For nearly four years our entire family and many of our friends had focused on Dana's condition and had prayed for her healing.

Now, a dumb, malfunctioning chair was distracting me from Dana herself. I would have never imagined that that could have happened—no more so than Peter imagined that he would deny Christ. But he did. And I temporarily got my focus off the most important thing in my life at that time—my daughter's health. How very typical that is of so many of us in our walk with the Lord.

Mary got it right! In her actions and her motives **AND** her focus! Mary had a sense—a feeling—that Jesus wouldn't always be dropping by, that one day soon he would be gone from her physical world. So she dropped everything and spent valuable time with Him. Martha couldn't understand Mary's focus!

The Lord wants us to work for Him, yes! But, first of all we were made to worship and love Him. Mary was sitting at His feet and enjoying his fellowship, and Jesus enjoyed hers! Martha was so distracted by her preparations and her actions that she failed to really comprehend who was there in her home. It was the Lord! The song I quoted earlier has this resolution: *"But if by death to living, they can thy glory see. I'll take my cross and follow close to thee."*

It's all about proper focus. Thanks Dana and "the chair" for reminding me of that important lesson!

Chapter 8
You've Got Dad's Hands

My husband was born during World War II while his birth father was overseas. During the time his father was away, my husband's mother became a Christian. It was a beautiful conversion that has led her to this very day as a beautiful Christian woman, admired by all her know her.

When David's father returned from the war, there were some things his birth father could not accept—mainly her Christianity. So while David was still less than a year old, his parents separated, and from that day to the day his father died, David never saw or heard from him. Life was not easy for my mother-in-law and a new baby living alone in California. Ultimately, they were forced to leave California and return to her father's home in Washington state.

Very soon my mother-in-law found shelter and comfort in a local Christian congregation who openly took her and

her young son into their hearts *and* their homes. She actually was so penniless after her divorce that she and David would live a few weeks or months with one family in the church and then another few weeks or months with another family. Long after we were married, the people of that local congregation still considered David "their boy."

When David was seven years old, his mother married his stepfather. Although David was now part of a "real family," life got harder in many ways. His stepfather was a very good man, but uneducated. He was a beautiful singer, though, and tuned pianos and sang for a living.

Theirs became a nomadic life that took the growing family from state to state

> ***Theirs became a nomadic life that took the growing family from state to state... living in a small, one room trailer.***

for several years, living in a small, one room trailer. His mother and dad would sing for revivals and special church services while his dad tuned pianos during the day. It was a meager existence, but I have never heard David or his mother complain about those days.

During the first five or six years of this new marriage, four children were born. With the birth of the fourth child, the family was forced to settle down—back in the State of Washington. David's mother went to work in a local mill, and his dad continued as much itinerant work as he could find locally tuning pianos and singing. Throughout this entire period of time, David and his mother never heard

from his birth father at all. The only information that he ever received was that his father had remarried shortly after the divorce and had another child—a daughter.

David matured, finished high school, and went on to college. This was a miracle in itself since his parents were so overwhelmed with responsibilities of the four younger children that it was all they could do to keep food on the table and a roof over their heads. Consequently, David never received any financial help from any one for college, graduate school, *or* postgraduate school. There just seemed to be a determination within him that drove him to these milestones.

After we married, David and I discussed his parents' divorce, and although I was very curious, David never seemed to want to pursue his birth father any farther than a passing discussion. Since we were starting our own family, he didn't want any confusion in our lives that delving into his past might possibly bring. And the years passed—over twenty of them.

Our oldest child was in college, and our second child was preparing to leave the nest for college as well. David had taken a new job in a different part of the country, but the kids and I were still in Washington getting things wrapped up for my move and getting both kids ready to return to college in California.

During this interval, I casually mentioned the situation of David's early childhood to a friend and told him that we knew that David's birth father had a twin, and that we even knew where he lived. Several times over the years, I had

tried to get some information about David's past but my efforts would only get so far, and then the door would close. My friend asked me if I would care if he called David's birth father's twin to see if he would give him some information. Surprise of all surprises! My friend reached David's uncle.

David's uncle was very cooperative; he told our friend that David's father had died the year before of lung cancer—only a couple hours' drive from where we were living. He told him the name of David's sister. She, too, lived only a couple hours in the opposite direction from our home. So, one night, the kids and I picked up the phone and called a total stranger who was my husband's sister. Over forty years had passed, and suddenly one night she received a call from her sister-in-law.

Cautiously, she answered my questions: Where had she been raised? What her childhood was like? etc. As the conversation progressed, she got more and more excited and animated, and we arranged to meet halfway between our two homes. So, on a beautiful summer Sunday evening, I drove east along the Columbia River Gorge; she drove west, and at a truck stop

> *...at a truck stop overlooking the Columbia, I met my sister-in-law for the first time.*

overlooking the Columbia, I met my sister-in-law for the first time. It was such a curious meeting; we talked and talked for hours it seemed. She had hastily gathered some family pictures of her father, and interestingly enough, our son resembles him a great deal.

Together she and I discovered several significant and somewhat uncanny coincidences. To begin with, her name is Kathie like mine, but that was only the tip of the iceberg. She had been raised her entire life by David's birth father and her mother as an only child. Over and over she had begged her parents to have another child—specifically, a brother! At last, when she was graduating from high school, her mother broke the news to her that she did have a brother, but that none of them knew exactly where he was.

The conversation became more coincidental as it progressed. The previous Easter holiday, our family had gone to Mount Bachelor in Central Oregon for a ski trip. At the exact time our family was skiing on Mount Bachelor outside Bend, Oregon, David's birth father was being buried in Bend.

Earlier that same summer, we had gone back to Bend for a summer holiday before we moved and the kids spread their wings to college. While our kids were out goofing around as teens do, David and I were sitting on the patio of a great lodge there. He remarked that he felt so at home that he would like for us to look for property to possibly retire in the area. In all the years we had been married, David had never said anything like that to me—not once!

That summer night while I was visiting with David's sister, she told me that his father had been a principal contractor on the construction of the very lodge where David and I had sat discussing our future just a couple weeks prior. Neither of us wanted to leave this "reunion." When we parted, we agreed that she and David would

communicate, and that hopefully, they would have an opportunity to meet at some point in the future.

The next summer when David and I returned to the Northwest for a visit, we made special arrangements for him to meet Kathie. She lived then in a small town on the Columbia River and worked for a car dealership there. Through some searching, we were able to locate her, and one very significant noon time, David and his sister and I lunched together at McDonald's. (It has always seemed curious to me that some of life's most significant experiences happen in the most common places.)

It was a tremendously emotional encounter—especially for Kathie—David's sister. She had been raised as an only child, lived a major portion of her adult life, and now she was meeting her big brother for the first time. As we all attempted to eat, she sat across the table from us in McDonald's and just stared. She was so full of information about David's birth father and so anxious to hear about our lives, children, etc.

There were several times during that conversation, however, that had deep meaning to me as I pondered the significance of her words. The words were significant to the occasion, but upon reflection they had a much deeper importance. She would stop mid-sentence and just focus intently on David. Then we would hear remarks like: "You have Dad's hairline." Or, "Your hands are just like Dad's." Or, "I can't get over how much you sound like Dad." Or, "Your hair is just the exact shade that Dad's was at your age."

As I sat there that day in a little-known town watching and listening to the first time meeting of a brother and sister who had never met in their entire lives, Kathie's words transported me beyond that place and time to a deeper level of implication and understanding.

In my Bible studies I had read and reread *John 14* for years. The first four verses have always made good sense to me. They have been a comfort and a promise to millions over centuries. Jesus was comforting His disciples and promising them that, although He would soon be leaving them in body, he was going to prepare a blessed place of rest and eternal

> **Not only did Jesus promise to prepare this place for us, but He promised to return and escort us back with Him.**

communion with Him and His father. Not only did Jesus promise to prepare this place for us, but He promised to return and escort us back with Him. What a consolation of hope; what a comfort to the grieving; what a hope when life crashes in on us with disappointment, despair, or illness.

But Thomas—the doubter—didn't get the next part of Jesus' promise. In *verse 5,* Thomas came straight to the point with his personal doubts: *"Lord, we don't know where you are going, so how can we know the way?"* Even though occasionally over the years I would begin to think I had a handle on the meaning of the rest of Chapter 14, more often than not I would return to the realization that I, too, was uncertain about Jesus' words. Jesus explains to Thomas *(verses 6-7): "No one comes to the Father except through*

me. If you really knew me, you would know my Father as well. From now on, you do know him and have seen him."

Thomas was puzzled, but Thomas was not alone! Philip interjected his "two cents" worth into the conversation: *"Lord, show us the Father and that will be enough for us!" (verse 8).* If you listen you can almost hear the frustration in Philip's tone of voice. He might have said, "Stop messing with our heads, Jesus. If you think we *know* the Father, just explain how this can be and show Him to us, and we will understand. It's as simple as that: just stop talking in riddles!"

For nearly three years Jesus had intimately walked and talked with these men; they had seen Him perform miracles; they had heard Him preach; they had watched Him live His life in a pure, sinless manner. And yet, they still didn't get it! Kindly, but rather firmly, and with a touch of divine impatience, Jesus explains to Philip and Thomas and to us one last time the nature of His divinity and the Trinity: *"Don't you know me, Philip, even after I have been among you such a long time? Anyone who has seen me has seen the Father. How can you say, 'Show us the Father?' Don't you believe that I am in the Father, and that the Father is in me?" (verse 9).*

I don't know if Christ's words made sense for Philip, but sitting at a plastic table in a McDonald's restaurant on the Columbia River witnessing this unbelievable first-time meeting of my husband and his sister, they began to make sense to me: *"To know the Son is to know the Father, and to know the Father is to know the Son."*

All my husband's life he had carried with him the characteristics of his birth father, but he had never been able to recognize them because he never knew his father. It took his sister to recognize the similarities; she was intimate with their father, so when she met his son, she instantly was able to identify his nature in her brother—the son.

Many lifelong mysteries about my husband were answered in that brief encounter. David has always been extremely gifted with his hands, both mechanically and in construction. His stepfather was a piano tuner and taught David how to tune and rebuild pianos, but when it came to building and repairing things, his step dad was definitely not gifted. Where did David get this ability? Not from Dave's mother; we knew that!

In the first church that David pastored in Southern California we built a new sanctuary using a great deal of volunteer labor. For over a year David was at the construction site night and day it seemed. One day the contractor asked him, "David, where did you get your training and experience in construction? I've never seen a minister who can do what you do with tools."

David's response was an honest one: "I've never had *any* instruction; I've just been watching you, following your example, and doing what you do."

The contractor was baffled. "That's unbelievable. You use my tools and approach this project as though it were second nature to you and as if you had been doing this type of work all your life!"

When we met David's sister, David discovered that his birth father had been a construction worker of journeyman status—that he was a skilled carpenter and cement worker. All his adult life, David had just been doing what came naturally for him, never knowing that his ability was an innate trait inherited from his father. It took his sister who knew the father well to identify their father's nature in him.

David has a quick sense of humor, and many say he is a natural comedian. There is no one in his family like him in that regard. His sister told him that their dad had always been funny and fun-loving and could always see something humorous in a situation and make people laugh. What a coincidence! Or was it? In reality, the nature of the father was being revealed through His son. Jesus continued His remarks to Philip in *verse 10:* *"...it is the Father, living in me, who is doing his work. Believe me when I say that I am in the Father and the Father is in me; or at least believe on the evidence of the miracles themselves."*

> **What a coincidence! Or was it? In reality, the nature of the father was being revealed through his son.**

Jesus wasn't a first century magician like David Copperfield sent to entertain the Israelites and divert their attention from the abuse of Rome! He was the living, incarnate Son of the almighty Father. The work He did was an indication of His divine nature. He didn't come to this earth to do a few little tricks, die a martyr's death, and then return from the dead Houdini style. Christ came to this

earth to redeem us from sin so that we could return to God's original design and commune with Him. He came to this world as the earthly embodiment of the divine nature to witness to us that God is real; He is flesh; He is alive; and He is forgiving.

God created us to have communion with Him; Christ communed with man to show man the very nature of the heart of God. When Christ's work here was over, He returned to the Father, but He didn't leave us alone. There is a third component of God's nature—His Holy Spirit. Jesus explained to Philip and Thomas and to us this incredible third attribute of the trinity *(verses 16-17): "And I will ask the Father, and he will give you another Counselor to be with you forever—the Spirit of truth. The world cannot accept him, because it neither sees him nor knows him. But you know him, for he lives with you and will be in you."*

After their initial reunion, my husband was able to visit his sister in Florida for nearly a week. It was the first time in their entire lives that they had had any quality time together. David shared with me when he returned how precious their time was. They just couldn't seem to get enough of each other; they stayed up late hours together just talking and getting acquainted. The amazing piece of it all, David said, was the instant ease and pleasure they shared in each other's company.

These two individuals, by all standards, are total strangers—casual acquaintances at best. What has made their relationship move to such a deeper level of communication almost instantly? Spirit! Without being

taught or without searching far and wide, the spirit of their mutual earthly father is in them both, and that has created a beautiful bond. *To know the father is to know the son, and to know the son is to know the father. And to know them both, is to recognize the Holy Spirit—the comforter.*

Our son flew to Florida as well to spend some time with his dad at his new aunt's place. Scott arrived in Florida before Dave, and together he and Kathie went to the airport to pick up David. Scott later shared with his dad Kathie's reaction when she saw David exit the plane.

Kathie was nearly jumping up and down, Scott said, as David walked from the little commuter plane to the terminal in Ft. Myers, Florida. She was saying, "I just can't believe it! It's like seeing Dad all over again; he walks just like him; he has Dad's hairline; his voice is even like Dad's. It's too uncanny to be true; I just can't believe it!"

Colossians 1:15 states it this way: *"He is the image of the invisible God, the firstborn over all creation."* And later in verse 19, Paul continues: *"For God was pleased to have all his fullness dwell in him, and through him to reconcile to himself all things..."* My new sister-in-law sees my husband as the image of their invisible father, and David's nature revealed all the fullness of a father whom she knew but who has been dead over ten years! It was David's actual physical body and his invisible spirit that reconciled the two of them in a bond that will forever remain.

So many people are looking for some visible sign of the Almighty—something or someone tangible that they can either see or feel and experience. Because God is more

often felt than seen, many people doubt His existence and look in the most ungodly places for the reincarnation of the Father. The puzzlement of those who *look* for the father is this: since they very rarely understand His essence, they don't recognize Him when they do see Him.

My sister-in-law had been raised by my husband's birth father, but she had never met my husband, and yet she was well acquainted with his father. My husband, on the other hand, was the son of the father, and yet never having seen him, failed to recognize within himself the reflections of the father that he innately bore. It took another child of the father—one who was well acquainted with the father—to see the resemblances.

For me that day, it was all too clear. I saw that afternoon the crucial obligation and privilege we as Christians have to witness. Our spiritual characteristics actually become images of the invisible Father for the people we encounter

> *Our spiritual characteristics actually become images of the invisible Father.*

throughout our lives. How can the world know who and what the Father is unless we truly bear His resemblances?

Two years after that reunion, my new sister-in-law and her husband accompanied us on one of our tours of Israel. In a hotel overlooking the Sea of Galilee, the four of us sat and talked. As we talked, tears streamed down Kathie's cheeks as she said, "I just can't get over the fact that *I* have a family. Just a couple years ago, I was all alone in this

world with no family but my husband and my son. Now I have an *old brother,* and all his family is mine as well."

Jesus is indeed our *old brother*, and when people accept His salvation, they are adopted into His forever family! As a born-again believer, fully surrendered to the Holy Spirit, it is inevitable that the evidence of a life-changing experience will be exhibited in my life. Then, when a world that is unacquainted with the Father looks at a Christian life they will be able to say, "Oh, I see now. That's what the Father is like. That's how a real Christian responds under extreme pressure. I see Him now because I see Him reflected through your life!"

Telling the lost about the Father is simply not adequate in and of itself. We must literally bear the resemblance of the Father so that when the world looks on, there is no doubt as to what the demonstration of His love shed abroad in our lives displays. It's not about us; it's about *"Christ in us the hope of glory..."* We, then, become the *"visible image of the invisible father."*

What a blessing it will be for you or for me someday to have someone look at us and say, *"Now I recognize the Father because you have His hands!* When you cleaned my house when I was sick; when you gave me a call when I was discouraged; when you picked up my kids after school when my car broke down; when you sent me a card when my friend died; when you brought me some groceries when my husband was out of work, I saw Jesus."

"...it is the Father, living in me, who is doing the work."

Chapter 9
Footmen or Horses

In my daily devotions as a college student, I stumbled across a scripture that has altered the perspective of my life. The weeping prophet Jeremiah was crying out to the Lord about the inequities of his life, comparing his life and its troubles to the seemingly successful and trouble free lives of the wicked nations around him.

Jeremiah was engaged in quite a dialogue with God about how unfairly God's people were being treated compared to the wicked nations around them. God responded to his cries of woe by zeroing in on the very core of his self-deprecation: *"If you have raced with men on foot and they have worn you out, how can you compete with horses? If you stumble in safe country, how will you manage in the thickets by the Jordan?" (Jeremiah 12:5).*

As a college student there was no way I could comprehend the full impact of those verses and what they were to mean throughout my life even to this very day. Yet sitting in a small student assistant's office adjacent to my

major professor, God seemed to speak to me. *"Kathy,"* He was saying. *"Mark this one down for it will have great significance in your life if you will let it."* No, His voice wasn't audible, but even to this day I can go back to that small campus in the sagebrush and take you to that little cubicle where He spoke to me. And so as much as I was able to comprehend then, I took note and began a mental journey that has been constantly with me through good days and bad, difficult years and fulfilling ones.

> *"Kathy," He was saying. "Mark this one down for it will have great significance in your life...*

That winter day I began to apply Jeremiah 12:5 as a water mark for the events of my life—a sort of mental test of my life against the Word if you will. As events began to march through my life with their predictable contrasts between happy and sad, good and evil, hopeful or desperate, and as life commenced its inevitable ebb and flow, I consciously labeled daily events and crises in my life as *footmen or horses.* From that formative time in my life, occurrences in my life (both crises and daily events alike) have been mentally categorized with this holy perspective.

Christmas of my junior year in college, my roommate and four other friends were in a tragic car accident returning to Southern California for the holidays. Two were killed instantly: one who was preparing to be a medical missionary, and the other was a friend who I had literally brought to our little Christian college. At first blush this was a *horseman.* There was no question.

My young life had been sideswiped in an instant. Just the night before I had talked seriously with my friend Sandy and helped my roommate pack to go home. Now, Sandy was gone! But in retrospect, it was much more a victory than a devastating blow. Who was this girl, Sandy?

The previous Christmas holiday when I had been a Sophomore, I ventured out on one of those excursions that only college students are foolish enough to attempt. I left my home in Spokane, Washington, and hitched a ride with an individual from our home church in Spokane as far as Fresno, California. There he left me at the home of some of his Christian friends who were total strangers to me. At midnight they took me to the bus station, where I caught a bus to Pasadena. Quite a way from Spokane!

My roommate lived in Pasadena, and she had told me that if I could get there, that she was "nearly certain" that she could get me a job working on the Rose Parade floats. Totally inexperienced in float building, but undaunted and full of the confidence of youth, I arrived in Pasadena. Janell, my roommate, pulled some strings, and by the next afternoon I was gluing chrysanthemums to Rose Parade floats. Just like that! This was a lark, and I was having a ball. Little was I to know that this was also a divine appointment preparing me for the first major testing of my adult life.

The second day of float making, Janell stumbled into an old junior high school friend, Sandy, who she introduced to me. Sandy was a cocky, smart aleck who had just been kicked out of a local junior college. Just off the cuff,

Janell and I together invited her to attend our little Christian campus in Southwest Idaho. We ended this invitation with this rather unostentatious invitation, "Our school doesn't care what you've done. They'll take anyone!"

Neither Janell nor I thought any more about this conversation, but a month later when we returned from my home in Spokane after the term break, there Sandy sat in the lobby of our dorm. She was over a thousand miles from home and in her rather sarcastic, perturbed way wanted to know why we hadn't been there to greet her!

Sandy was tough, and she had had no formal exposure of any kind that we could tell to the gospel or the restrictions of a conservative Christian campus in the sixties. She began to make her own way and move in her own circle of friends, but there was something winsome about her. Much to everyone's surprise, she returned the next fall. So what had she and I talked about so seriously the night before she died?

I was one of the dorm "leaders." The very night before she died, Sandy had been called before our awesomely serious dorm council for sneaking out of the dorm after hours with some of her new found friends. I was extremely uneasy and unusually quiet during that meeting, for it seemed that her eyes were literally piercing me as she glared at me as though I was the one who had betrayed her. It was a busy night with preparations for the holidays, but my heart was heavy as I returned to my packing.

How could I have been caught in the middle of this mess? Finally, late in the night, I told Janell, "I just can't

go home until I settle this with Sandy." And so I went upstairs to her room. She and I stepped out in the hall, and although the years have blurred the memory of the specific words of that conversation, the tone of it remains in my heart. I went away with a lilt to my step and a song in my heart, for somehow God witnessed to me in that brief encounter

> *...although the years have blurred the memory of the specific words of that conversation, the tone of it remains in my heart.*

that, as much as Sandy understood, that her life had been changed! And I knew that Sandy and I had settled any differences we had between us.

Was her passing a horseman? Of course! Her loving family was robbed of her at an early age; there was so much that they would miss. There would never be a wedding or grandchildren or shared holidays or shared family crises. But in another sense, this was *not* a horseman. I had done the best I knew; my life had made a difference; and I would see my friend again someday. No, and this is said with no intention of minimizing my friend's life and death, but this could not be a horseman. It was a serious "footman," but not a horseman.

And so I began to progress through my adult life, categorizing events in relation to Jeremiah 12:5 and endeavoring to keep them in proper perspective. As time has passed—over thirty-five years now—I have visited and revisited, studied and reexamined that passage numerous times and in multiple situations. This passage has literally become my lifetime word study.

"If you have raced with men on foot and they have worn you out..." What a mouthful! Do you hear how God is responding to Jeremiah's pleading with Him regarding the apparent comfortable conditions in which the wicked are living? Jeremiah had done exactly what so many of us do in life. He had taken His eyes and thoughts from Jehovah God and had begun to *compare* his life with the wicked.

Jeremiah seems to feel a compulsion to remind God of what is going on here in His earth and how well the wicked are doing in comparison to the people of God. *"Why does the way of the wicked prosper? Why do all the faithless live at ease? You have planted them, and they have taken root; they grow and bear fruit. You are always on their lips but far from their hearts"* (Jeremiah 12:1b-2).

Poor, pitiful, complaining, comparing Jeremiah! He continues in the very next verse to remind God how righteous he has been. You can almost hear his whining echoing down through the ages. We've all said the words; we might as well admit it!

> **Poor, pitiful, complaining, comparing Jeremiah!**

It's not too difficult to hear ourselves in Jeremiah: "Why does nothing bad ever seem to happen to my neighbor when he never goes to church or never pays his tithe?" Or, "I raised my kids in a Christian home, and to the best of my knowledge and ability, I provided them all the opportunities and the loving environment needed to become a Christian. But despite all my efforts, they have gone out into a sinful, wayward life and are living a life of compromise far from

the Father's house. Why has this happened to me?" Or, "Why does my neighbor who drinks and cheats on his wife and taxes get the raise that I so rightfully deserve?"

And on and on and on the endless list of comparisons continues. Complaining and comparing and whining had become a way of life for Jeremiah. And it has become that for many Christians today.

Jeremiah even had the gall to offer some suggestions to the Lord about what He could do with these wicked people: *"Drag them off like sheep to be butchered! Set them apart for the day of slaughter? (Jeremiah 12: 3b).* And if that isn't audacious enough, Jeremiah rants on in verse 4 by giving God his own explanation for why bad things are happening. He blames all the bad in the world on the wicked people who are living in his neighborhood.

Sounds familiar, doesn't it? "If we had lived in a different school district, my kid would have never been influenced by such a wild crowd!" Or, "If my family hadn't ventured out on the highway that day, the accident would have never happened." Or, "If we had purchased another house in a different neighborhood, my husband would have never met the neighbor lady who he eventually had an extramarital affair with."

And then Jeremiah makes his gutsiest allegation of all when in confidential tones he reminds the Lord what people are saying about him: *"He will not see what happens to us, " (verse 4).* What nerve! It's easy for us to take a rather self-righteous view of this statement and reproach Jeremiah. How dare he tell God Himself that the people don't think He cares!

Perhaps this is what Jeremiah himself was thinking, and he was laying the blame on the people. Jeremiah was the prophet. He should have been the very one to give the people strength and confidence and remind them that God was in ultimate control, but he was a weak whiner, and at that time at least a puny, pitiful model of a spiritual leader.

Once again, this is not too far from today! As *good* Christians we are tempted to make remarks like Jeremiah said the people were saying. "God doesn't ever seem to answer my prayers. I don't think God remembers my name, much less my address." And just like He did then, God gets fed up with our complaining and comparing and whining and self-pity.

Enter **Verse 5!**

It becomes a matter of perspective and keeping our eyes on Him! To paraphrase God's response, He's saying something like this to Jeremiah: *"What are you thinking, Jeremiah? If these little daily irritations that come your way make you so bitter and full of complaints, how will you respond when something really gigantic enters your ministry and you are compelled to deal it? Get a grip! Get over it! This is what is called life!"*

It's like comparing a hangnail to cancer! There is no comparison; these two things aren't in the same ball park. They're not even in the same league! They are horsemen or footmen. No sane person would attempt to enter the Kentucky Derby and race against the horses, but some would attempt to run in the New York City Marathon.

And as if that tongue lashing isn't enough, God continues his reprimand to Jeremiah: *"...and if you stumble in safe country, how will you manage in the thickets by the Jordan" (Jeremiah 12:5b).* Jeremiah reminds us of a playground tattletale, telling God just what all the people are saying about Him. God must have been embarrassed for Jeremiah that he would stoop to such levels.

The flood time of the Jordan generally happened at harvest. Living in the bushes and thickets along the river were wild animals, including lions! When the waters flooded, the wild animals would be forced from their dens and lairs and would spread out over the countryside waging death and havoc on man and beast alike.

Now, it comes into focus for Jeremiah. He understood the hazards of being caught in the thickets along the Jordan's banks during flood time. Or being anywhere in the proximity of the Jordan during that season for that matter! Jeremiah was familiar with the Jordan River Valley. He must have known its destructive powers and respected them.

By now Jeremiah must have been thinking, "Enough already! I get the picture!" He must have been humiliated, embarrassed and humbled as God brought his complaining

> *Jeremiah must have been thinking, "Enough already! I get the picture!"*

and whining into crystal, clear focus and perspective.

What was God saying to Jeremiah, and what is He saying to us? *"What's wrong with you? You're familiar with this old river; this isn't a flood, it's just a little spring*

rain. This crisis is nothing; in the scope of things it's insignificant! Once or twice in your life this old muddy river is going to flood; you need to get hold of yourself and look at this situation and see what it really is. If you fall apart over this, you'll never make it when a real flood comes!" It's a matter of perspective!

This little verse is the Christian's lifelong measuring stick, a continual standard. Is my situation a footman or is it a horse? Is this a spring rain or is this the big hundred years flood? Is it necessary for me to lengthen my stride and improve my endurance, or do I need to get out of the way rather than be trampled? Can I recognize this storm as the gentle spring rain that the crops so desperately need, or is it imperative that I scramble with all the rapidity I can muster to higher ground?

God continues in the ensuing verses to remind Jeremiah of all the wicked ways of the people. Jeremiah was well aware of this in the first place. Why was this necessary? Sometimes God needs to remind us that He knows. He's got this whole deal in perspective, and He has it all in control. If it's footmen, we'll be able to compete. If it's horses, He will be with us. If it's just an ordinary day, He'll be with us; and when real crisis comes our way, He is there as well.

Finally, God makes a promise to Jeremiah, and that promise is extended to us even today. *"And if they learn well the ways of my people and swear by my name, saying 'As surely as the Lord lives' ...then they will be established among my people," (verse 16).*

God is reminding Jeremiah that it isn't his job to worry about all these heathens who are prospering in the land. If the wicked come to Him and swear by His name, He will have compassion on them and accept them into His forever family, and if they don't listen, He will destroy them. All in His own time.

And so we return to the footmen and horses. Many events in my life never even made the cut for consideration for either of these categories. They were just events of life! That's a healthy view. But some things, were they footmen, or were they horses? It's a matter of perspective.

One Saturday morning in San Diego when both of my children were babies, I received a wake-up call from Albany, New York that I will always remember. Both of my parents had been injured in a serious car accident and neither was expected to live. Was that a footman or was it a horse? What was that call? On the surface, it sure looked and felt like a horse.

> **Both of my parents had been in a serious car accident and neither was expected to live.**

I flew to Albany for ten days and left my babies with neighbors while my parents suffered from broken backs and serious neurological damages. My mother was on a *Streicher* frame and couldn't move. (A *Streicher* frame is a modern torture device on which a patient is literally *flipped* every two hours to keep from getting pneumonia.) My father was on a separate floor and wing of that huge research

hospital. Ten days were spent traveling between the two of them, staying with total strangers, talking to doctors, and at the young age of twenty-eight, representing my entire family in important medical decisions.

Once I was even sent into the operating room with a phone for my mother to talk to my dad because her blood pressure had fallen so low; they were concerned that she might not make it. At the time, that was one fast moving horse. But God was merciful, and both my parents survived and are in their eighties today.

Instead of that event being a melancholy memory, it is an ever-present reminder of God's protection—a reminder of the wisdom God gave me that surpassed my years, a reminder of the love extended to me by a group of strangers who allowed me and my parents to be Jesus to them for a few days. It is an event laced with precious memories of God's healing and protecting power. The ramifications of that accident have followed my parents into their old age. But they haven't made them bitter or complainers; they have served as reminders of God's love.

A year and a half after my parents' accident, I received another phone call. This time the call was from the American Red Cross in Songkla, Thailand. My younger brother who was a Peace Corps volunteer there had been in a terrible motorcycle accident. This call was an inquiry as to where his body should be sent when he expired.

Now, that's a no-brainer! That's a horse! That's the hundred years flood for sure! This was my little brother— the one who had the world by a string. The handsome one

with the half inch long eyelashes. The one who could sing like a bird. The one who had just graduated from college with a 4.0. Why would

> **Wasn't that enough for one family? Enough's enough!**

God allow this to happen to my brother? Didn't He know that my parents were still in "rehab" from their wreck? Wasn't that enough for one family? Enough's enough!

A week and a half later I received yet another phone call. This time the call was from my brother himself. He was calling me from Honolulu saying he would be landing in Los Angeles in a few hours and asking me to meet him at the plane. He was injured all right, and seriously! He had received multiple head and facial wounds and had undergone brain surgery in a Baptist mission hospital in Thailand. His face was disfigured, and the brain injury would cause him to have a lifetime of serious health problems. But he was alive! And with life, there is always hope! He couldn't go home because my parents were in no real condition to care for him so he lived with us for one entire year. What a year that was!

While staying with us, he underwent extensive reconstructive plastic surgery to his face, and with these surgeries he began a lifetime of adjustments. Yes, in many respects this was and has been a horse! But my brother's life has been one of great blessing. He has turned his understanding and knowledge of the Eastern cultures into a lifelong mission. He has ministered all over the United States, even returning to Thailand for a time to minister to the Thai people. He never dwells on his injury or the way it changed his life. This *horse* refocused his life and filled

him with a compassion and love that he might have never know before. So, for him, was that a *footman* or was it a *horse?*

On and on the parade of life has passed. And although there have many events and happenings that in their initial essence appeared to be horses, in the final analysis they were only footmen. There was the day several years ago that was probably the darkest we had ever faced. In a political move made by some who hadn't attended our church in years, our loving congregation asked my husband to leave after he had pastored there for over seven years.

> *...although there have many events and happenings that in their initial essence appeared to be horses, in the final analysis they were only footmen.*

That was a horse for sure. No one believed it; we were all in a stupor. People and pastor alike. The few who had caused the havoc were celebrating, but God's church was devastated! My husband could have appealed the decision and won! In many respects the whole incident was a farce and went against denominational "rules." In retrospect, we've wondered more than once why he didn't appeal. But he didn't, and what started out to be the biggest flood of our married life, both for us and for our children—a flood that nearly swamped us and sent wild creatures of all types from their dens and into our territory—has brought us some of the greatest blessings of our lives.

Without a doubt, that was a tragedy in our lives that brought us pain beyond all verbal expression. Yet we can't nor would we go back and redo that one day. It's over! God has had his final say of judgment for some of those individuals, and He continues to bless our lives as we continue to serve Him. A horse, yes; this was a flood—one of the "hundred year" category. But, one that God's grace has helped us to survive and to survive with joy and hope for the future.

It's all a matter of perspective. It's how we look at the things that happen to us; it's not the things that happen to us. I would not be honest if I said or even implied that we haven't asked some of those same questions that Jeremiah asked. (Jesus Himself asked, "Why?") In asking why, though, we set Him free to begin the healing process in us. He never promised that we wouldn't have horses or floods in our lives. But if we can't deal with the ordinary day-to-day happenings that come into our lives, we will be trampled or swamped and flooded when the real crises come.

Psalms 37 is God's beautiful reminder of His constant protection as we remain within His "cycle of victorious living." The Psalm is explicit: Fret not! Trust! Delight! Commit! Rest! Those words are so easy to let roll off our tongues, but they create a difficult concept to live. That is, it we are attempting to live them alone! After this beautiful cycle of commitment, the Psalmist, David, continues with this incredible promise of hope for tomorrow, *"I was young and now I am old, yet I have never seen the righteous forsaken or their children begging bread," (Psalms 37:25).*

What's in your life today? Can you categorize it? Is it a footman or is it a horse? Is it the regular spring rain or is it the swelling of Jordan? God wants to empower you to face—and face with victory—whatever comes your way.

The Apostle Paul encompasses our entire range of human feelings in familiar and indomitably rewarding words for the faithful believer: *"I have fought the good fight, I have finished the race, I have kept the faith. Now there is in store for me the crown of righteousness, which the Lord, the righteous Judge, will award to me on that day—and not only to me, but also to all who have longed for his appearing" (II Timothy 4:7).*

Chapter 10
Things Aren't Always as They Seem!

Things aren't always as they seem! I have driven across the great American Southwest on a hot day and followed a mirage endlessly—always anticipating some shade that never materializes. It appeared as though there should be water and shade a few miles down the road. But the forces of nature played an optical trick on my psyche, making me imagine that the shimmering light I saw down the road would provide a needed respite on a hot, dusty drive. The more I traveled, though, and the faster I drove to overtake this phenomenon of nature, it continued to elude me. It just wasn't what it seemed!

Sometimes events can happen in our lives that appear one way to the outside spectator. On more careful observation and examination, they are indeed totally different than they appear at the initial casual observation.

This was made comically clear to me a few years ago during the Christmas holidays. My husband and I had

"honeymooned" for two subarctic days at Sun Valley over thirty years prior. At the time neither of us skied, and I doubt that we would have skied anyway on a two-day honeymoon.

Regardless, a few years ago after we began to ski together, we had fantasized and discussed how much fun it would be to return to Sun Valley to ski. My parents live in southern Idaho, so my husband and I, and our two grown children returned to "Grandma's house" for Christmas. That year our plans were made to take our long awaited ski trip between Christmas and New Year's.

On our honeymoon, David had rented a little cottage, but this time we decided to stay in a nice lodge and enjoy the skiing for a least three days. Our daughter lived in New York City, and when she learned that we had a ski trip planned to Sun Valley—well, you guessed it! She wanted to go with us.

The morning after Christmas 1997, we put our son back on the plane to return to his home and job. The three of us set out for Sun Valley in our rented car for a great "family" time together. It wasn't the original trip that David and I had planned, but when your family is distant, any time together is cherished.

> *We shelved our romantic notions about this time in Sun Valley and altered our plans to make it a "family time."*

Therefore, we shelved our romantic notions about this time in Sun Valley and altered our plans to make it a "family time."

The first day on the slopes of Sun Valley began with promise. We had our skis, but we had to rent Dana's equipment, purchase lift tickets, and study the trail maps. At last, after all these preparations, we were set to go. The day was cold and crisp, but the runs were well-groomed. It promised to be a tremendous time for the three of us.

Over the years, our family has developed a "ski pattern." David and our children are all moderately good skiers, but mom—now that's another story. Nobody complains that I slow them down, though, because it is so incredulous to anyone who knows me that I would even be on a pair of skies—an athlete I'm not! Here's the pattern: David takes off straight down the mountain like a bullet, and sooner or later when I get my courage collected, I begin to laboriously snowplow my way down the mountain. Finally, another family member will follow a few seconds after me.

Although the scheme has never been articulated, it's clear, and the unspoken message is understood by us all: *Keep Mom from getting hurt or hurting someone else, and be there for her if she needs assistance.* A reasonable distance down the run, David will stop and wait for me to overtake him, check to see if I'm all right, and then we usually finish the run in tandem. Whoever was following me in the first place will generally go streaking by about this time. It's our system, and it works! The family tolerates my caution and slowness as a trade-off for our being together.

That day was no different. David took off down the mountain, lickety-split; I followed, and Dana brought up

the rear. This pattern was working beautifully until the third run of the day. The more I ski, the more confidence I amass, and that particular day, I was doing pretty well—even if I say so myself. David was out of sight, and I was cruising along by myself, manipulating an advanced blue run. It was the third run of the morning, so I knew the turns and angles, and with each slope, I was getting better and more aggressive.

As I was making a sharp right turn *and* going down a steep slope simultaneously, it happened! A hot dog skier came roaring down the hill behind me, caught the back of my ski with his, and before I even knew what was happening, I was cascading head over skis down the mountain. I landed face forward in an ice bank and crashed with such force against the ice that for a moment I saw a bright light and felt a warm glow.

Generally, my experience is that a skier like this would be an adolescent, but to my amazement, a grown man screeched to a stop and inquired if I was hurt. I have had my share of falls and spills skiing, but I've never been hurt. This time, I knew, was different. When my assailant asked me if I was hurt, I answered, "Yes, I believe I am." When he heard me say this, he turned away and transformed into a blue streak going straight down the mountain. That was the last I ever saw of him!

Dazed and stunned, I lay there in the snow bank, taking a mental tabulation of my physical condition. Much to my surprise and relief, it appeared that no bones were broken, although I could tell already that my body would be sore—

and soon! What seemed to hurt the most was the area of my face around my eyes and nose. As I lay there in the warmth of my own shock, Dana skied down the mountain and stopped beside me. She helped me to my feet, collected my skies and poles that were strewn down the mountain like the wake of a giant storm, and together we limped to the bottom of the run where David waited unsuspectingly.

I must have looked pretty "shook up," and by now my head ached like the aftermath of one giant hangover. (I've actually never had a hangover, but none could be any worse than how I felt at that moment!) Apparently, my goggles had smashed into the bridge of my nose, and they were pushed into my face, making my face absorb the full weight and intensity of the fall.

David and Dana purchased me something to drink, located some headache pain reliever, and sat with me in the lodge until I was less disoriented. They went back and took a couple runs together, and finally convinced me that if I didn't get back out on the mountain that day, I might never ski again. So I did. Only one run, however. My ski trip terminated with that fall.

Before nightfall I had the beginnings of not one, but two, black eyes. The bridge of my nose was swollen, and I was beginning to look a mess. Actually, I was miserable! David and Dana finished the next day or so of the trip, and then we set

> *Before nightfall I had the beginnings of not one, but two, black eyes.*

out in our rented car to return to the Boise airport. Our plans were to fly to the Portland area to spend some more time with our son and visit my husband's family.

Dana was staying in Boise a couple days with friends, so we dropped her by their place before we arrived at the airport. By the third day after the "accident," I had two royal shiners. They were both beauties! Black and blue and green and yellow—an entire rainbow of colors splashed across my face. If there had been a contest for the most disfigured and miserable looking face that week, I certainly would have been a contender for the top prize!

And so, in this condition, I arrived with my husband at the Boise airport. To our surprise, my elderly parents had driven to the airport to see us off, and they were shocked and horrified at the condition they found their only daughter. As we stood in line to get our boarding passes, we attempted to explain to my parents what had happened. When we got to the ticket counter, though, we were faced with a typical holiday air traffic dilemma—our flight to Portland had been cancelled.

That was okay with me. I didn't feel like traveling anyway. My parents were right there, and I could rest at their place for a while until a plane was available. But that wasn't okay with my husband! Our son had purchased tickets for the two of them to attend the Portland Trailblazers game that night, and that was "Priority Number One" for him! David was persistent with the ticket agent, and finally made a believer out of him that he MUST find him a flight to Portland.

The ticket agent went through all the computer gyrations he could think of until he located two tickets—one through Spokane, arriving in Portland in enough time for David to attend the Blazer game with our son, and the other through Salt Lake City, arriving in Portland later in the evening. We agreed to split up and take separate flights, but there was a hitch—the flight through Spokane was leaving in TEN minutes—not even enough time for my husband to check his baggage!

Right there at the ticket counter in front of the agent, my parents, scores of other travelers, God, and everybody, David grabbed his suitcase, quickly threw it on the floor, opened it, and began taking personal items out that he would need for the evening in case I didn't make it to Portland. And then he made a mad dash for the flight that was already being boarded.

As David was dashing toward his plane's gate, he tossed the rental car keys toward me and said, "Here, you can take the car." And with hardly a "good bye," he was off in a sprint. There I stood—apparently beaten and abandoned—standing in the middle of the Boise airport obviously being comforted by my parents. There were dozens of sets of eyes on me. Other travelers looked at me with a combination of pity for me personally and abhorrence for the monster of a man who had just left

> *There I stood—apparently beaten and abandoned—standing in the middle of the Boise airport obviously being comforted by my parents.*

me in such a woeful plight with only my aging parents to care for me. At least he had given me the car!

That's the way it must have looked, but *things aren't always as they seem!* Jesus life and words are abundant with incidents and accounts that were totally misunderstood by the judging religious leaders and the public alike:

> Residents of Nazareth *thought* Mary was an immoral young woman, but God had chosen her to be the virgin mother of his son, Jesus. *Things aren't always as they seem!*

> Mary and Joseph *thought* that Jesus was being a disrespectful twelve-year-old when he disappeared in the temple, but he was really exercising his role as the Son of God. *Things aren't always as they seem!*

> The Pharisees outwardly *appeared* to do the right things, yet Jesus penetrated their facade and identified who they *really* were—a generation of snakes and vipers. *Things aren't always as they seem!*

> The rich young ruler *appeared* as though he was acceptable by doing all the politically correct things, but he failed to comprehend that salvation is by *grace* and not by *works. Things aren't always as they seem!*

> Nicodemus *thought* Jesus was asking him to do the impossible, but Jesus only wanted him to be

willing to humble himself to be His follower. *Things aren't always as they seem!*

Nazareth *should have* given Jesus the "keys to the city," but instead they rejected him because they failed to recognize who He really was. *Things aren't always as they seem!*

Mary and Martha *thought* Lazarus should be healed, but Christ didn't choose to heal a sick man; rather, he chose to raise a dead one! *Things aren't always as they seem!*

The disciples on the Lake of Galilee were *confident* Jesus was insensitive to their fear of the storm, but Jesus was more concerned about building their faith than with the building storm around them. *Things aren't always as they seem!*

Jerusalem *saw* a lame man by the Pool of Bethesda looking for movement in the water in order to walk, but Jesus saw a man who could walk if he only believed. *Things aren't always as they seem!*

The disciples *thought* the young boy's lunch provided limited resources to feed the crowd, but Jesus wanted to use this little lunch to prove that with Him, "little is much!" *Things aren't always as they seem!*

The disciples *saw* a racial and gender stereotype in the Samaritan woman at the well, but Jesus saw a woman who desperately needed the love,

forgiveness, and grace of God. *Things aren't always as they seem!*

And then one day, the religious rulers got the best of this man called Jesus. And they crucified him. That *should have* taken care of that, but it didn't! *Things aren't always as they seem!*

Three days later on a crisp morning just as the sun was rising, the Son rose. And with this resurrection, time was divided!

Because... things aren't always as they seem!

What a lesson for us today! We are not the judge; we can't see the future. And we certainly do not know the entire past of all the people and situations over which we so righteously pass judgment.

In a previous chapter, I mentioned a little about my husband's childhood. By most people's standards, it was extremely impoverished. He was abandoned by his father before he was even born, and his father never saw him once in his life. He and his mother were forced to live at the mercy of loving people in their local church until his mom married his step dad. Then they lived from town to town and state to state for several years, living out of a tiny travel trailer.

David was often kept home from school to baby-sit while his parents worked. When he was a little kid, he broke out a front tooth that his parents couldn't afford to have fixed. He doesn't recall ever having any new clothes. In

high school he worked three jobs after school just to be able to have a few of the things his parents couldn't provide.

The house that David's step dad purchased was almost condemned when he bought it. It was at the end of a dead end street, and it was a unique merger of two small houses shoved together with a bathroom between. Not the best neighborhood in town to say the least!

But the summer after David had graduated from high school his wise and insightful pastor came to their home and told Dave's parents that they *must* find a way for him to attend college. They all were "dumb" enough to trust their pastor and put David's life in God's hands. With only $90.00 and no hope of any parental help, David set out for a small Christian college campus. This was most likely one of the best and most significant decisions of his young life. Largely because of this move, God has blessed his life in abundant ways.

> *They all were "dumb" enough to trust their pastor and put David's life in God's hands.*

A few years ago David and I attended his twenty-fifth high school reunion. The reactions of his classmates were comical. They just couldn't get over it! No one had expected David to amount to much; most of the really popular kids had stayed right there in that little Northwest mill town and worked in the paper mill. The majority of them have had marriages that have disintegrated, and many of them hadn't attended college—much less received two post graduate degrees.

This isn't about education or college degrees. It's about perception and judgment. *Things just aren't always what they seem.* Most of David's high school classmates never even gave him a second thought after graduation. After all, he was the poorly dressed kid from the run down house on the back side of "prune hill, *"Man looks on the outside, but God looks on the heart!"*

History is replete with accounts of people who made the wrong judgments. There is one notable entry in the journal of King George of England, made on July 4, 1776: "Nothing of significance worth reporting happened today." Was he ever wrong!

God is the judge of the human heart and life. Our place as Christians is to keep our human judgments out of the way and allow people to become what God wants them to be—to reach their fullest potential for Him. If only we could comprehend the magnitude of this.

In our judging, we limit others and stifle God's creativity in them. God help us to keep our opinions to ourselves and allow our friends and loved ones to reach the full potential that God has for them. We judge in so many ways—gender, racial, social, cultural, financial. We need to keep our hands away from all of these judgments and let God work! Then, when someone else in the Kingdom "succeeds," we are all winners. For, we are *"workman together for Christ!"*

And remember: *Things aren't always as they seem!*

Chapter 11
Sweat Equity

If our family history were to be equated with driving a car, 1989 would have to be remembered by all four of us as the year of the big crash. In a previous chapter, I wrote about *footmen and horses*, and indeed most of the happenings that had crossed our pathway we had been able to legitimately, and with God's grace, label *footmen*.

A few times we have had to swerve quickly or apply the brakes with split-second reflexes, but 1989 wasn't just a fender bender, or a sideswipe. Emotionally, financially, relationally, spiritually—in every way, it was a head on collision—one that nearly took us all out! Without God's grace in our lives, this *horse* in our lives could have wiped us totally!

Actually, we had been cruising along with typical road hazards, but overall we had felt God's protection and safety. An occasional bump here, a detour there, delayed traffic over at another spot. My husband had been pastoring our congregation for six years, and the last two of those six

had been the smoothest and the best. Yet, when he had accepted the call, he knew full well that it was a potential disaster.

In the fall of 1982 my husband accepted a pastorate in a distant state from where we lived. Although he had been forewarned that the church was in trauma, he felt God leading him there just the same. When we arrived we found a congregation stunned and much-divided from a long history of events. The hard feelings were not directed toward my husband, but nevertheless, he was the new pastor challenged with dealing with all the ramifications and fallout that comes from a church disaster. So, he began the task at hand with *He began the task at hand with a spirit of optimism and a sense of God's direction.* a spirit of optimism and a sense of God's direction.

God was faithful. Within a couple years, the church had recovered the numbers (both financial and numerical) that had been lost, we had four full-time staff members, and there was a new prevailing spirit of optimism. The church grew in all ways, people were excited, the programs of the church were healthy, and the people seemed to love and want to follow the leadership of the pastoral team.

And then after over six years, the crash came! One October Sunday in 1988 when it was time for my husband's three year review required by his denomination, the unexpected happened. The denominational procedure has changed since then, but in that year, a pastor could be asked

to leave if the congregational vote was even one vote under two thirds. And that is exactly what happened! Two votes under two-thirds, and my husband was out of a job! In other words, the minority was in control. This was the identical treatment received by the previous pastor! To this day, many of the people who came to vote "no" that day do not attend even that church. Their names were on the rolls, so they came to have their say!

And so it was that our world crashed in around us. In the spring of 1989, my husband was finishing his doctoral studies, I was in a master's program, our son was a sophomore in college, and our daughter was a senior in high school, anticipating college in the fall. We were cruising along, and then CRASH! Our world changed as we knew it, and to this day it has never been the same.

We were assured by all the local and general church leaders that my husband would be reassigned. Month passed anxious month as we waited, but the "call" never came. It appeared to us as though we were now damaged merchandise. For six months, my husband continued to be employed by that congregation, but that was indeed the most rapidly passing and the most apprehensive six-month period in our lives together.

Our daughter was home with us which allowed us to bond with her and face this tragedy together as a team, but our young son was at college a thousand miles away. His world as he had known it was falling apart. There was no tangible support available to him that we could feel coming from any direction at such a vulnerable time in his life.

When the six months of promised employment had passed, and the new assignment was not forthcoming, my husband was forced for the first time since he left seminary to take a secular position. God was really faithful, and for a short time David worked for a local man writing a sales program. This man promised to match my husband's salary, but after three months, his funds were depleted, and that employment came to an abrupt stop.

So, we borrowed. And then, we borrowed again! My husband did weekend supply pastoring. I took a summer job working in a neighboring church office. The kids worked at the usual summer part time jobs available to college students. For the first and only time in our marriage, we did financially "desperate" things like getting a month's extension on our car payment. We borrowed from our insurance; we borrowed from our parents; in retrospect, it seemed as though borrowing was going to "bleed us dry!"

Toward the end of July, my husband was offered a position teaching in a Christian university in a southern state. The pay was less than his pastoral salary, but the school offered tuition remission for our kids at a sister college. Altogether, God had answered our prayers. The pain wasn't over, but the healing process had begun. And three years later, David accepted another position at a different southern Christian university.

So, in the fall of 1992, three years after we had left the Northwest, we found ourselves in Nashville, Tennessee. Both of us had good jobs, but financially, we were a mess. During all the years from 1988 through 1992, we had

faithfully met our monthly financial obligations, paid our tithes without exception, kept the kids in college, and endeavored to maintain a semblance of normalcy. But we knew that our credit card debt was extensive, and although our credit was good,

> *...although our credit was good, we couldn't foresee any way at all to get back into the housing market and reestablish ourselves financially.*

we couldn't foresee any way at all to get back into the housing market and reestablish ourselves financially.

We had purchased our first home in 1976, and from then until 1989, when we were forced to sell our home in the Northwest, we had owned our home. We had been renting for three years now, and we knew from a good economical standpoint, that we must invest in a home. There was no way, though. Who would loan us money? Our credit was good, but our debt was astronomical. We were a financial liability to any lending institution. Basically, all we had left was our good name and character.

And so, foolishly, we began to shop for property in Nashville. It was impossible, but it didn't cost anything to look. We visited every conceivable area of Nashville in general proximity to my husband's work, driving hundreds of miles, studying neighborhoods, and weighing possibilities. Nothing seemed possible. Our knowledge of the real estate market had taught us that new construction would give us the most return for a few dollars. And at our ages, we felt that was paramount.

Finally, we settled on a new development consisting of what most real estate agents refer to as "starter" homes. The agent must have surely

> **The agent must have surely thought by our ages that we had come to purchase a home for one of our children—CASH!**

thought by our ages that we had come to purchase a home for one of our children—*CASH!* These homes were much smaller and more modest than we had owned, but we swallowed our pride and gingerly entered the model homes office. Nearly instantly, we bonded with Jim, the salesman. He liked us and was extremely creative in working with us.

It was possible to get this modest little three bedroom home for only 5% down, but we literally didn't even have that much. We cashed in our current life insurance policies for whatever was left on their face value. (Three years prior in our "borrowing era," we had borrowed against them extensively so there wasn't much equity in them, but there was a little.) This transaction provided us some unexpected cash, but not enough. Actually, it gave us only half of the minimum down required—2.5%. Still not enough!

It was at this juncture that we first heard the term *sweat equity.* Jim, our salesman friend, told us that at one time his company had allowed potential buyers who were shy of the minimum down to literally "work" their way into the house by doing all the interior work. Naively, we jumped all over that. We could do that! We weren't too proud. If it meant a few nights of painting to get back into a house of our own, it was worth it!

Our hopes were dashed, however, when Jim returned with the news from his parent company that they had discontinued that policy. Too many people had done too poor of a job, had procrastinated, or attempted to cut corners, that the company just didn't want to mess with the policy of *sweat equity* anymore.

My husband, however, is a good salesman. He presented our case again, and somehow he made a believer out of Jim that we would not disappoint them—that we were different. David must have been convincing, and Jim must have been equally convincing to his superiors, because my husband prevailed with his bid to get the balance of the down payment by this process called *sweat equity*.

We entered into an agreement with a real estate developer to do *all* of the interior painting and trimming of the entire house—*SWEAT EQUITY*—actually more sweat than equity! This particular house had massive amounts of crown molding, and it must have had a hundred doors—all of which had to be painted and primed on both sides! In addition, there was an oak fireplace that had to be stained.

Not only did we agree to do all this painting, but it was also part of the agreement that we would purchase all the paints and supplies. On the surface this looked and felt doable, but when the builders had the house ready for our part of the work, it was the dead of winter. There was no electricity in the house, and it was freezing cold outside.

We began the work during Christmas break when our daughter was home from college, and together the three of us leaped into the task at hand with an abundance of

enthusiasm and a corporate spirit of, "We can do this; surely, two weeks would be ample time to complete this project!" We purchased a propane heater to keep our work areas semi-warm and tackled a massive task.

I remember the first night that we worked. After a few hours, I drove to a Chinese restaurant and brought a meal back for the three of us. We sat down in the middle of the floor and had a little banquet by the propane heater. A few nights later, our daughter remarked to us, "You know, Dad and Mom, that first night when you bought the Chinese dinner, I thought this was rather enchanting, but now this is just hard work!" And she was right!

After several days Dana returned to college in Southern California, and David and I both had to return to work as well. Now, the only time we had to work was the evenings. They were dark and long and cold. David gerrymandered a way to rig electricity from the contractor's temporary electrical box on the street. We brought in extension cords with floodlights, wore gloves, coats, and boots. And we continued to paint!

Each afternoon before it got totally dark, we would rush to the house to see the previous night's work in the daylight so that we could touch it up appropriately. The work dragged on and on. Finally, we hired a friend to help us get the job done. At one point we borrowed extension ladders from a construction crew in order to get to the high areas we couldn't reach with the ladders we had purchased.

At last, though, the job was done! On a cold, icy day in mid-February we moved our furniture from storage into

our brand new home, and for the first time in over three years, we became homeowners again! What a feeling of accomplishment! *Sweat Equity* had gotten us

> **What a feeling of accomplishment! Sweat equity had gotten us over the top;**

over the top. It was the necessary ticket we had to purchase to get us back on the road financial solvency. But it wasn't a free ticket.

We have learned numerous critical spiritual lessons in all of this—lessons that are invaluable! They are so invaluable, in fact, that as a writer I am willing to reveal some of the most intimate and painful experiences of our journey in order to allow you, the reader, to share in the joy that comes through suffering! My story—our story—is really no different than yours. The events and circumstances are different; the places aren't the same; the people are dissimilar; but the emotions and deep feelings are the same. It is a story of pain, a story of life's disappointments—a story of life itself!

It has been well over a decade since this "crash" in our lives, and we have deliberately kept a silent vigil. Our silence hasn't been out of a sense of embarrassment or humiliation, although those are factors in the loss of a dream. Some of these years have been lonely and desolate ones as we repeatedly have asked the Lord, "Why?"

Our silence, however, has been deliberate—it has been fueled and driven by the conscious determination to allow this "tragedy" a seasoning time. There is no redemption in

bitterness or finger pointing or rancor. Paul said it well: *"...We are hard pressed on every side, but not crushed; perplexed, but not in despair, persecuted, but not abandoned, struck down, but not destroyed" (II Corinthians 4:8)*

There is no growth without pain, and there is no growth without somehow having a human willingness to bond our puny efforts with his divine greatness. Romans 8:28 is still in the Bible: *"And we know that in all things God works for the good of those who love Him who have been called according to his purpose."* How many times have I wished that that verse would vanish from the Word? This would give me license, then, to point fingers and lay blame and justify why life has not been fair. I would have license to suspend my efforts to rebuild a crashed life, to never attempt to get up again, to just quit! If only Romans 8:28 would vanish. That would do it!

Many lives are similar to ours. We are just cruising along, seemingly on cruise control—enjoying the scenery— and then, **CRASH!** We are unexpectedly sideswiped by the sudden, untimely death of a loved one—a death that nearly annihilates us and separates us from God's amazing love. Or a marriage that began with such promise and high hopes for a beautiful future is shattered by one partner's actions. Or, our own body is afflicted by an incurable or crippling disease which forces us to reroute our lives. Or, you are in a situation like ours where your "dream" is shattered and you stand exposed before your peers, and justification and explanation appears to look like defensiveness to most people.

For a while friends and family are there, and then little by little, they get absorbed in their own lives, and we are left alone. It is in these times that we ask, "How/why could something like this happen to me? I haven't done anything wrong; I don't deserve this." It is at this juncture that we have an option. We can choose to be bitter and angry and resentful, or this aloneness can drive us *to* the Heavenly Father. When we are in the Father, we are indeed never alone for His loving arms are always there to comfort and hold and uphold us.

So where does *sweat equity* enter into all of this? What we *do* is *never* enough! It just isn't! God expects us to contribute the *sweat* and do everything we humanly know to do to resolve the situation. But when all our efforts are expended, and we stand exhausted and incomplete before Him, exposed and vulnerable, He freely and generously provides the equity from the abundant supply of His inexhaustible resources! We cannot work hard enough or long enough or sincerely enough to earn it! We don't merit it; there is nothing that any of us could ever accomplish or attain that makes us worthy of this equity. But when we have accomplished all that we can do with our measly human efforts, He dumps in all the *equity* that we need. The heavenly bank confirms our loan because we have become partners with Christ Jesus.

And that equity is God's amazing grace. Ephesians 2:4 explains it like this: *"But because of his great love for us, God, who is rich in mercy, made us alive with Christ even when we were dead in transgressions—it is by grace you have been saved, through faith—and this not from*

yourselves, it is the gift of God—not by works so that no one can boast. For we are God's workmanship, created in Christ Jesus to do good works, which God prepared in advance for us to do."

> *He giveth more grace when the burdens grow greater.*
> *He sendeth more strength when the labors increase.*
> *To added affliction He addeth His mercy;*
> *To multiply trials, His multiplied peace.*
> *His love has no limit; His grace has no measure;*
> *His power has no boundary known unto men.*
> *For out of His infinite riches in Jesus,*
> *He giveth and giveth and giveth again!*

Chapter 12
A River Runs Under It

A nd so what is this all about? What is the importance or value of all these stories about an ordinary woman and her family? Nothing really, and everything totally! These are stories of God's faithfulness through the ordinary days and through nearly insurmountable times. They are stories of finding *joy beneath the pain.*

For several years I have nurtured this idea and reality of suffering in the lives of Christians. It is such a personal and intimate subject, and yet it is so close to where we all live. It speaks all languages and reaches all lands. Suffering touches us all at one time or another. In one way or another, we are all affected by it.

The question as believers is to understand the nature and reason for suffering in our lives. The simple answer, *"It rains on the just and the unjust,"* simply does not pacify or soothe us when we are literally bleeding and dying from hurt, abandonment, and anguish. And many times our

Christian friends appear to us to be the most disinterested, unconcerned, or judgmental.

Even those of us who are "mature" Christians know that our ultimate strength comes from the Lord, but in our hours of pain, we can be lonely and confused. Unless we can honestly reach the core of the issue of suffering in this world, we can become bitter with little hope for a future.

Suffering and pain come into our lives because something is wrong—extremely wrong! Suffering can be the result of something or someone else, or it can be self-inflicted. Nevertheless, it is suffering, and we are never *whole* until we adequately deal with the *hole* in our heart. And that's exactly what it is—a hole! It is as though a bullet were targeted directly at the most vital part of our humanity, and that it struck with amazing accuracy.

Surprisingly, we are alive—critically, but to our chagrin and dismay—not mortally wounded. At times we feel that it would be easier and a lot less painful to be dead than to deal with this merciless, incessant suffering! We stagger and stumble through our days in our own daze, never recognizing that God is at work in this suffering as well as in the good times of life. Our intense pain becomes a lack of life and vitality rather than impetus with growth and survival.

> *We stagger and stumble through our days in our own daze...*

When we face our pain honestly and respond to it appropriately, we begin to find real joy beneath that pain. This seems to be a paradox, but the Bible and the testimonies of

millions of lives give real and positive witness to this truth! There are some critical facets about suffering and the contemporary formulas that are freely and glibly distributed to the bleeding and suffering. The message oftentimes seems to be that as Christians we should just "get over it and give it all to God." It's just not that simple when you have been sideswiped by some of the events of life discussed in the last chapter: loss of a loved one, divorce, personal illness, financial loss, or loss of a dream.. These crises are *real* and *painful*, and they take *time* to heal.

When we begin to understand the reasons for pain, then we can develop an access pathway to the ultimate joy that lies beneath it. Pain comes to us for many different reasons. First of all, pain is in the world because Adam and Eve disobeyed and sinned. When we admit that there is sin in this world, we admit the amazing proclamation of redemption for this world. This is the *much more* solution of God's amazing grace. Suffering because of our sin is spiritual and requires a spiritual solution. Recognizing the spiritual cause of some suffering frees us to accept the amazing spiritual solution. The great hymn that we love to sing says this better than any words I could pen:

> *Marvelous grace of our loving Lord,*
> *Great that exceeds our sin and our guilt.*
> *Yonder on Calvary's mount outpoured—*
> *There where the blood of the Lamb was slain.*
> *Grace, grace, God's grace.*
> *Grace than will pardon and cleanse within.*
> *Grace, grace, God's grace.*
> *Grace that is great than all my sin.*

I John 1:9 is a verse that we love to quote, but we have difficulty applying: *"If we confess our sins, He is faithful and just to forgive us our sins and to cleanse us from all unrighteousness," (KJV)*. Do you comprehend the amazing import of these amazing words? We simply *cannot* suffer over confessed sins! When we continually nurture and obsess over confessed sins, we propagate a theological error. When God forgives our sins, the Bibles says that he casts them in the deepest sea *"as if they were no more!"*

Do you get it? God is a gentleman, and when he says He forgets, He does just that. He doesn't charter a boat and sail to the middle of the ocean, sink a sonar device, and begin looking for the pinger of our spiritual black box. When He forgives our sins, it's a done deal. We remember, but He never does.

But, you say, I'm confident that I haven't sinned. Why is God exacting this unbearable suffering on me? There are numerous other reasons besides "sin," that cause suffering in this world: We suffer because God is disciplining us; we suffer because of the sins of others; we suffer from thorns in the flesh; we suffer from rejection of those who would have us do wrong; we suffer from isolation and loneliness that comes from being set apart; we suffer from errors in judgment; we suffer as a testimony of our faith; we suffer from disasters and senseless tragedies; we suffer in life's seasons; and we suffer when love is not returned.

It is unwise and even foolish to pursue suffering, but the truth is that in one form or another, it will reveal itself in all our lives. Regardless of whether we are presently able to recognize it or not, joy is indeed beneath all the

suffering of life. God's very character—His indisputable, spotless character—is the collateral that makes this amazing joy available and accessible! Joy is a *spiritual* substance available to all believers. It is everlasting and it overflows to others around us. This world can never offer or imitate what is of the spirit. There are some astounding counterfeit attempts, but they never match or even approach the amazing joy that comes from Him!

What then, as believers, do we do with this pain and suffering that invades our lives, stalks our emotions, and sabotages our very life itself? We study His Word and act on its truth. Then, once we have identified the source, we can begin to righteously and humbly recycle the pain. There may be days and months and even years when a pain is too raw, and the memories

> *What then... do we do with this pain and suffering that invades our lives, stalks our emotions, and sabotages our very life itself?*

and questions are too near the surface to process. But with God's grace we still can claim Romans 8:28!

As we process our own personal pain, we can begin to see ways to recycle it and make it suitable for the Master's use. As we process this pain, little by little, we remove our own personal obstructions to joy. Joy is never created or fabricated. We simply remove the obstructions of pain and suffering in our lives that have layered over it. We never search for joy outside the love of God; we remove our own personal barriers and obstructions to His joy and ever so slowly begin to access what has been there all the time.

Many believers fail to accept God's warmth and thus refuse to access His unbelievable joy. They allow themselves to feel overwhelmed with a sense of helplessness and lack of control over their own lives. This is a self-contrived trap! We literally become trapped in our own sense of grief and despair, and being trapped is a great place to hide. As we choose to be obedient and access God's amazing joy, we choose not to be trapped.

When I was four years old, my parents moved our family from San Antonio, Texas to Fairbanks, Alaska. That was a serious move! The majority of my childhood—until I was a young teenager—was spent in Alaska. Over the years I have discovered that my friends and acquaintances have some sort of fascination with this type of a childhood; they tend to romanticize it, but to us it was ordinary. We were remote and far from home, the winters were bitter, cold and severe, but this was my childhood, and I really had no awareness that this extreme sort of existence wasn't "normal."

> *I have discovered that my friends... have some sort of fascination with this type of a childhood; they tend to romanticize it.*

A great deal was normal for us that I later discovered was far out of the ordinary for others. We had snow from early October until late April, and this snow was accompanied by nearly unbearable thermometer readings— once as low as 63 degrees below zero! One winter the downtown district of Fairbanks caught fire, and ultimately a large portion of the businesses burned because the water

literally froze in an arc as it sprayed from the hoses! With only our eyes showing, my brother and I wore three complete layers of clothing to walk two blocks to school! It was not uncommon for grown men to be forced to leave the territory permanently because they failed to take necessary precautions against the cold and suffered frostbite of their lungs.

One thing that we all enjoyed and anticipated in this amazing north land was the Winter Carnival. This carnival was the precursor of the Iditarod dog sled race that now has become world famous. The carnival took place after Christmas, and it was unfathomable to the "outsider." Usually, the weather hovered between 20 and 30 degrees below zero for this annual "outdoor" event. Although this carnival was patterned after the traditional county fair or town carnival, it took on some unique qualities of its own.

The entire city and surrounding areas turned out to watch the Eskimo blanket toss competition and the dog sled races. The Eskimo women sat cross-legged on their blankets demonstrating how they chewed caribou hides to make the soles for their mukluks. It was quite a cultural event! We would be bundled up, but we would all be there. Since we lived in Alaska during the Korean Conflict, there would always be a massive military presentation. One year several hundred paratroopers and all their equipment and vehicles dropped from the sky! What a colorful and captivating sight for a little girl from Texas.

As unique as this might seem, the most unique part of the Winter Carnival was that it took place *on* the river. That's

right, *on* the river! And that's not all that happened on the river in the winter. We drove our cars on the river. Everyone did! The shortest distance between two points is always a straight line, and when the river is frozen solid nearly to its very bed, nothing stops any vehicle from traversing it. We drove on the river, but we were always aware that it was a river. We knew that when the spring breakup came, this frozen ice highway would take on a totally different form.

A few summers ago, my husband and I visited Fairbanks, and I had the opportunity to revisit many memories of my childhood. We saw my school and home and church and other landmarks. It was a great trip down memory lane. But one of the most enjoyable things we did on our summer jaunt was to ride a large 300 passenger paddle boat down the river on a tourist excursion. It was a gorgeous day; the sky was a royal blue; trees and flowers were in full bloom; and the temperature was 90 degrees above zero! What a contrast!

This was the very same river that I had *driven* on as a child with my father. How was this possible? The spring and the breakup come despite the coldness and repressible conditions of the Arctic winters. Just as surely as winter arrives each fall with all its fury, each spring warmth will return that melts these rivers of ice. This warmth is followed by flowers and blue skies and balmy weather—God's respite from the severity and cruelties of equally harsh winters.

As I was enjoying a matchless afternoon as a tourist on one of the great rivers of the northland, my thoughts returned

to this concept of pain and joy. Pain is like the ice of the rivers that piles up and covers all the joy of life. But beneath that ice, there is always a river. The river doesn't leave, it just changes form for a season. And then the spring comes. And with that spring returns hope and warmth for yet another season.

What does the Word have to say about suffering and pain and joy? *"In this you greatly rejoice, though now for a little while you may have to suffer grief in all kinds of trials. These have come so that your faith—of greater worth than gold, which perishes even though refined by fire—may be proved genuine and may result in praise, glory, and honor when Jesus Christ is revealed. Though you have not seen him, you love him; and even though you do not see him now, you believe in him, and are filled with an inexpressible and glorious joy, for you are receiving the goal of your faith, the salvation of your souls" I Peter 1:6-9.*

Our suffering provides us impetus for self-review. Trust must be invested in Him, and suffering gives us an opportunity to be utterly dependent on Him. Life is then viewed from an eternal perspective. In our suffering we can demonstrate Christ's power to draw others to Him. Our suffering forces us to look at God rather than at ourselves and our circumstances.

There is no comfort compared to the comfort by which He comforts us; there is no freedom like the freedom to trust Him; there is no confidence like the confidence we have to trust Him. When we as Christians suffer, the knowledge of his love can become greater than the discomfort of our suffering, His grace can be greater than

our disgrace, and our gain in Him can become greater than any earthly loss.

Christ's resurrection is the forever proof of that joy, for just as the spring breakup follows the frigid Arctic winter, joy can always follow pain, and Christ indeed has born all our pain! Beneath the pain and suffering of life, there is always the availability of the Joy of the Lord! He is ever-present! He doesn't go away. Life, though, with its inevitable disappointment and pain can sometimes cover up and layer over the joy until we somehow feel that His joy is no longer accessible.

We commence this incredible and surprising journey called life, and before we know it, we stumble. We never really intended to; something just came across our pathway, and we tripped. The one we trip over most is ourself! But we *can* get out of our own way and let the Lord guide and direct us. It is possible to walk through the events and seasons and passages of life without stumbling over ourselves! God's joy is accessible and available. It is ever present, and it overflows! Just as the great rivers of the Arctic freeze solid enough to become a winter highway, the burdens and pressures of our own lives can blanket and mask God's amazing grace and His constant joy. But like the flowing river beneath the ice, He is there in all life's seasons. He is waiting to assist us in removing the layers of life and access His amazing joy!

We CAN walk through life without stumbling over our selves!

Vessel Ministries II Corinthians 4:7

I am interested in more information about Kathy Slamp's speaking and tape ministry.

My name is _____

Address _____

City/State/Zip _____

Phone _____

Email _____

Group I represent _____

• •

I am interested in information about Kathy's other publications. Please send me information regarding:

Reflection Profiles _____
(a Bible study series)

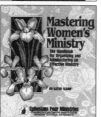

Mastering Women's Ministries _____
(a women's ministry manual with audio tapes)

You may contact Kathy at:

Kathy Slamp
Vessel Ministries
253 Breezy Pointe Ct.
Wichita, Kansas 67235
(316) 729-2597
Email: dkslamp@cs.com